SO-COO-946

Spike Lee

by **Laurie Lanzen Harris**

LUCENT BOOKS
A part of Gale, Cengage Learning

GALE
CENGAGE Learning™

Detroit • New York • San Francisco • New Haven, Conn • Waterville, Maine • London

LIBRARY OF CONGRESS CATALOGING-IN-PUBLICATION DATA

Harris, Laurie Lanzen.
Spike Lee / by Laurie Lanzen Harris.
    p. cm. -- (People in the news)
Includes bibliographical references and index.
ISBN 978-1-4205-0344-9 (hardcover)
1. Lee, Spike--Juvenile literature. 2. Motion picture producers and direc-
tors--United States--Biography--Juvenile literature. I. Title.
PN1998.3.L44H377 2011
791.43'0233092--dc22
[B]
                                                            2010028700

Lucent Books
27500 Drake Rd.
Farmington Hills, MI 48331

ISBN-13: 978-1-4205-0344-9
ISBN-10: 1-4205-0344-8

Printed in the United States of America
1 2 3 4 5 6 7 14 13 12 11 10

Printed by Bang Printing, Brainerd, MN, 1st Ptg., 12/2010

Contents

F ame and celebrity are alluring. People are drawn to those who walk in fame's spotlight, whether they are known for great accomplishments or for notorious deeds. The lives of the famous pique public interest and attract attention, perhaps because their experiences seem in some ways so different from, yet in other ways so similar to, our own.

Newspapers, magazines, and television regularly capitalize on this fascination with celebrity by running profiles of famous people. For example, television programs such as *Entertainment Tonight* devote all of their programming to stories about entertainment and entertainers. Magazines such as *People* fill their pages with stories of the private lives of famous people. Even newspapers, newsmagazines, and television news frequently delve into the lives of well-known personalities. Despite the number of articles and programs, few provide more than a superficial glimpse at their subjects.

Lucent's People in the News series offers young readers a deeper look into the lives of today's newsmakers, the influences that have shaped them, and the impact they have had in their fields of endeavor and on other people's lives. The subjects of the series hail from many disciplines and walks of life. They include authors, musicians, athletes, political leaders, entertainers, entrepreneurs, and others who have made a mark on modern life and who, in many cases, will continue to do so for years to come.

These biographies are more than factual chronicles. Each book emphasizes the contributions, accomplishments, or deeds that have brought fame or notoriety to the individual and shows how that person has influenced modern life. Authors portray their subjects in a realistic, unsentimental light. For example, Bill Gates—the cofounder and chief executive officer of the software giant Microsoft—has been instrumental in making personal computers the most vital tool of the modern age. Few dispute his business savvy, his perseverance, or his technical expertise, yet critics say he is ruthless in his dealings with competitors and driven more by his desire to maintain Microsoft's dominance in the computer industry than by an interest in furthering technology.

In these books, young readers will encounter inspiring stories about real people who achieved success despite enormous obstacles. Oprah Winfrey—the most powerful, most watched, and wealthiest woman on television today—spent the first six years of her life in the care of her grandparents while her unwed mother sought work and a better life elsewhere. Her adolescence was colored by promiscuity, pregnancy at age fourteen, rape, and sexual abuse.

Each author documents and supports his or her work with an array of primary and secondary source quotations taken from diaries, letters, speeches, and interviews. All quotes are footnoted to show readers exactly how and where biographers derive their information and provide guidance for further research. The quotations enliven the text by giving readers eyewitness views of the life and accomplishments of each person covered in the People in the News series.

In addition, each book in the series includes photographs, annotated bibliographies, timelines, and comprehensive indexes. For both the casual reader and the student researcher, the People in the News series offers insight into the lives of today's newsmakers—people who shape the way we live, work, and play in the modern age.

A Talent for Film and for Controversy

O ver the course of his twenty-five-year career, Spike Lee has become the most prominent African American filmmaker in the country. Since his first commercial film, *She's Gotta Have It,* appeared in 1986, he has released nearly a film a year, and nearly every one has dealt with questions of race, identity, relationships, and politics. While his movies have always sparked debate among critics and audiences alike, they have also won Lee wide praise—and criticism—for their provocative subject matter and tone, and for what some believe to be his habit for courting controversy.

Lee has spent a lifetime defining what it means to be black in America. His inspiration came in part from his own upbringing. His mother was a teacher of African American literature and art, and his father was a jazz musician. Both parents instilled in Lee and his four siblings the importance of art, and of the African American contribution to the nation's cultural heritage. He took their teachings to heart, following in his father's and grandfather's footsteps to one of the finest traditional black colleges in the country, Morehouse, where he found his calling as a filmmaker.

His films are powerful, provocative explorations of African American life in its many aspects, from the personal to the political. He explores the personal lives of black Americans in movies like *She's Gotta Have It,* which portrays modern sexual mores in the black community; *Jungle Fever,* which takes on the topic of interracial romance; and *Crooklyn,* which is a reflective, sentimental look at growing up middle-class and black in Brooklyn.

Lee has made many films with overtly political messages as well. *Do the Right Thing* is a powerful portrait of a black neighborhood descending into chaos after the death of a black man at the hands of the police. *Malcolm X* presents the life and work of an African American icon, describing the journey of the fiery preacher for the Nation of Islam from separatism to reconciliation during the most crucial years of the civil rights movement. In *Clockers*, Lee depicts the horrors that crack cocaine wreaked on the urban black community, and *He Got Game* shows how young black men are exploited by the world of big-time sports. In *Bamboozled* Lee takes broad, satiric aim at the way African Americans are portrayed in mainstream movies and television shows. In the film *Miracle at St. Anna*, he pays respect to a black battalion from World War II, revealing how they were victims of racism despite their selfless service to their country.

Spike Lee, center, acted in and directed his first commercial film She's Gotta Have It *in 1986.*

These same films represent another, equally important aspect of the work of Spike Lee: Whether praised or panned, his films spark controversy, inciting contentious discussions in the media and among film audiences. The most famous of these controversies surrounded two of his best-known movies, *Do the Right Thing* and *Malcolm X*. When *Do the Right Thing* was released, the *New York Times* convened a panel of critics and politicians, hoping to defuse an outpouring of racially motivated violence that never took place. Before the release of *Malcolm X*, the studio that produced the film insisted that Lee screen the film for the local police force. Once again, no racial incidents occurred. Lee responded by condemning critics and politicians alike for refusing to discuss what he felt was the message of his films: that racism continues to exist in America and should be central to any discussion of the culture.

Lee received three Emmys, including one for Exceptional Merit in Nonfiction Filmmaking for his 2007 documentary, **When the Levees Broke.**

Lee's films have inspired other controversies, too. Some women felt that Lola, the central character of *She's Gotta Have It*, was little more than a sexist stereotype of a black woman. *Girl 6* was nearly universally condemned for its depiction of female sexuality. And many critics condemned his characterization of the Jewish club owners in *Mo' Better Blues* as vicious and anti-Semitic. Lee was baffled by these accusations at first, then responded with characteristic condemnation of those who dared to accuse him.

Lee's knack for controversy has also led him to engage in very public and contentious battles with other directors, including Quentin Tarantino, Clint Eastwood, and Tyler Perry. Each of these confrontations has been about matters of race and of these directors' depictions of African Americans, which Lee finds demeaning and insulting, a situation he feels impelled to comment on and to correct, if he can. Similarly, he has taken on some of the biggest names in gangsta rap, condemning the creators of music and especially videos that he feels demean black people and glorify a life devoted to outlandish displays of consumerism.

Lee's independent streak, while making him controversial, has also led him to make savvy business decisions. While still in his twenties, he started his own film production company, 40 Acres and a Mule, to allow him greater artistic freedom and control over his work. Over the years, it has grown to become a major force in movie production. Lee also began a long and lucrative career as a director of commercials, starting with a series of popular ads for Nike, in which he costarred with legendary basketball player Michael Jordan. He later developed a partnership with a large advertising agency which guaranteed him both autonomy and a larger financial stake in the proceeds from the ads. This combination of creative and business acumen is rare in any business owner and is further evidence of the independence and vision of his work.

Over the past twenty-five years, Lee's fortunes have risen and fallen. Some of his movies have received great reviews and great box office receipts; others have been dismissed by critics and ignored by audiences. Through it all Lee has continued to create films that showcase his many talents, including two outstanding documentaries, *4 Little Girls*, about a 1963 Birmingham church bombing that killed four black girls, and *When the Levees Broke*, about the devastation of New Orleans by Hurricane Katrina. Both documentaries were praised for their thought-provoking, eloquent portraits of two key events poised at the intersection of race, politics, and history in America.

Fiercely intelligent and independent, notoriously prickly and provocative, Spike Lee is as fascinating as the films that have made him a star. He is a pivotal figure in modern American cinema, a man whose vision and art will never be compromised by what others expect of him or by any attempts to define him.

Chapter 1

Becoming Spike

Spike Lee was born Shelton Jackson Lee on March 20, 1957, in Atlanta, Georgia. He is the eldest of five children and has three younger brothers, David, Cinqué, and Chris, and a younger sister, Joie. His father, William "Bill" Lee, was a jazz musician, and his mother, Jacqueline Shelton Lee, was a teacher of art and literature. It was Jacqueline who gave her eldest son his nickname, Spike, saying he was "a tough baby," but also to reflect his grit and the legendary stubbornness that have helped him become one of the most successful and outspoken film directors of his generation.

The Lee family moved from Atlanta when Spike was a toddler, first to Chicago, then to New York, where the family settled in Brooklyn, the setting for many of his films. They first lived in the Crown Heights neighborhood and later moved to Cobble Hill, where they were the first African American family on the street. It was there that Lee first experienced racism: "First couple of days, we got called 'nigger' by some kids," he recalled. "Once they saw that there wasn't a hundred other black families moving in behind us, like we're the only one, then it was O.K. and it was never an issue after that."[1] In 1962, the Lee family moved again, this time to the predominantly middle-class black neighborhood of Fort Greene. His block had lots of kids who played together until the street lights came on, not worrying, as kids do now, about their safety. "I never had to worry about getting into fights, or think 'Am I going to get hit by that errant bullet?'"[2] he says.

Spike with his father, Bill, attend a screening in 2009.

A Young Life Steeped in African American Heritage

Bill and Jacqueline Lee raised their children to respect their African American heritage, a legacy revealed in their own careers. Bill Lee played the upright bass with several New York jazz ensembles and also appeared on studio recordings with a wide range of musicians, including Judy Collins, Bob Dylan, Josh White, and Odetta. Spike recalls his father introducing his children to the best in jazz, emphasizing its importance as an African American art form, and taking them to the finest concerts and finest venues in jazz. "My father would take us up to the Newport Jazz Festival," he recalls. "Or, if he was playing at the Village Vanguard or the Bitter End, sometimes we could stay up late and go with him,"[3] Lee remembers, referring to two of New York's legendary jazz clubs.

Bill Lee's career took a downward turn in the 1960s, when electric bass began to replace acoustic bass in performance and recordings. As stubborn as his son, Bill Lee refused to play the electrified version of his instrument, which he thought was inferior in tone, quality, and artistic expression. As a result, the family's finances suffered, and Jacqueline went back to work as a teacher of art and African American literature at a private school in Brooklyn. She had raised her children to love the work of black American writers, and Spike remembers it well. "I was forced to read Langston Hughes," he recalled. "And I'm glad my mother made me do that."[4] She also shared with them her love of theater, museums, and movies, and the family took part in all the cultural life New York had to offer.

Going to School

In choosing where to go to school, Spike also made decisions based on his African American heritage. Unlike his siblings, he chose not to take the opportunity to go to the private school where his mother taught—and where the students were mostly white. He chose instead to attend the local public schools, where most of the kids were black. He graduated from John Dewey High School in 1975 and went on to Morehouse College in Atlanta, one of the finest historical black colleges in the country. He was the third generation of his family to attend the storied school, following his father and his grandfather. His grandmother, who lived in Atlanta, paid for Spike's college education; she lived close enough to campus that he ate dinner with her nearly every night, returning to the dorms to sleep. He has nothing but praise for the supportive role she played in his life: "It was my grandmother who put me through Morehouse, then [New York University] film school, plus she gave me additional funds for my films.... She wasn't rich at all—she just saved her social security checks and gave it to her struggling first grandchild."[5]

Lee thrived at Morehouse. During his freshman and sophomore years, he worked for the school newspaper and the school radio station, where he hosted a jazz show. But then tragedy struck. During Lee's second year of college, his mother,

Jacquelyn, was diagnosed with liver cancer. She died in 1977, when Spike was twenty. His aunt called him with the news, which he described as "the worst words a human can hear." He felt her loss deeply and says that for several years "I had recurring dreams where I had conversations with my mother—she would come to me and we would talk."[6]

The summer after his mother died, Lee started to experiment with film for the first time. He had received a Super-8 camera the previous Christmas, and he wandered around New York, capturing life on film. During the blackout of 1977, looters took to the streets, and Lee recorded it all. When the dance craze known as the Hustle had people dancing in the streets, he captured that, too.

When Lee returned to college that fall, he had decided what his major would be: mass communications, with a concentration in film. He took his film classes at nearby Clark College, which shared courses and faculty with Morehouse, and learned the basics of movie making. Lee studied film with a particularly demanding professor, Herb Eichelberger, who required his students to shoot, edit, and present their films in the span of just one week. Lee recalls that that regimen made him incredibly focused and helped him determine his career path.

Professor Eichelberger encouraged Lee to take the material he had shot in the summer of 1977 and turn it into a film. Called *Last Hustle in Brooklyn*, it featured the looting and the dancing he had captured earlier. Lee is embarrassed by the low quality of the work now, and no copies are available. But it did get him noticed. Eichelberger continued to encourage him, and he gained confidence to pursue a career in film.

Lee graduated from Morehouse in 1979 and spent the following summer working as an intern at Columbia Pictures studios in California. He wanted to go to graduate school in film and took a look at the top film schools, including the University of Southern California (USC), the University of California at Los Angeles (UCLA), and New York University (NYU). He settled on NYU and moved back to New York to begin serious study and training for a career in making movies.

Spike Lee worked for the school newspaper and radio station at Morehouse College.

A Personal Rift

When Lee returned to New York to live, he moved in with his Uncle Cliff, not his father. Just a year after his mother's death, in 1978, Bill Lee had remarried. His new wife, and Spike's stepmother, was a white woman named Susan Kaplan. Lee claimed the remarriage created an irreparable rift between him and his

An Early Love of Sports

Most of Spike Lee's fans know of his love of sports, especially his enduring devotion to basketball and the New York Knicks. He remembers loving to play and watch sports, whether it was neighborhood street games or organized activities. As a young boy, he dreamed of becoming a professional athlete. He and his brother Chris loved attending New York Mets games, and he thought his dream job would be to play second base for the Mets. By high school, he knew that his size and his abilities ruled out a professional career, yet he kept playing and was always a leader.

A classmate from high school remembers him: "Even in the ninth grade at John Dewey school, everything was about sports, baseball and basketball especially. The funny thing is that Spike wasn't the best athlete, but he would always be captain."

Spike Lee: That's My Story and I'm Sticking To It, as told to Kaleem Aftab. New York: Norton, 2006, p.12.

father, caused in large part by Kaplan, who, Lee claimed, made him and his siblings unwelcome in their own home. "In retrospect, I blame my father," he told his biographer, Kaleem Aftab. "He could have stopped her from systematically kicking all of us out of the house, but he didn't. And one by one, we got the boot."[7] Although Bill Lee was the composer for several of Spike's later films, his remarriage changed their relationship forever. To this day, they remain somewhat estranged.

NYU, *Birth of a Nation*, and Birth of a Film Career

In the fall of 1979, Lee began graduate school at New York University's Tisch School of the Arts, one of the top film schools in the country. His classmates included such future giants of the industry as Ang Lee, who would go on to create films like *Crouching*

Tiger, Hidden Dragon and *Brokeback Mountain,* and Jim Jarmusch, the creator of *Stranger than Paradise.* The difference from Morehouse was striking, too. With Ernest Dickerson, Lee was one of only two African Americans in the first year of the film program, and they did not feel welcome. "Ernest and I were not welcomed with open arms," he recalls. "Not by the faculty, nor by the students. A lot of people thought that we were there for the quota, to make up numbers so NYU could get their federal grant money. So we knew that, in order to succeed, we had to be five, even ten times better than our white classmates. But we knew right away that we belonged. All we wanted was the equipment."[8]

As part of their first-year classes, NYU film students view and study what are considered some of the classics of the history of film. One of those movies is D.W. Griffith's *Birth of a Nation*, a silent film from 1915 that depicts the South during and after the Civil War and celebrates the Ku Klux Klan (KKK) in the rebuilding of the South in the Reconstruction era. Even though Lee recognized Griffith's importance to the history of filmmaking in his technique, he was appalled that the blatant racism of the work was not part of the academic discussion. "They taught that D.W. Griffith is the father of the cinema," he says. "They talk about all the 'innovations'—which he did. But they never really talked about the implications of *Birth of a Nation*, never really talked about how that film was used as a recruiting tool for the K.K.K."[9]

In reaction to the work, Lee submitted a film, *The Answer*, as a freshman project. It features a young African American screenwriter who is assigned to remake *Birth of a Nation* and is a pointed rebuke to Griffith's picture. The screenwriter, unable to write the movie, is attacked by Klansmen, and in the film's final shot, he faces them, ready to do battle.

The Answer was a galvanizing piece of filmmaking at NYU. Some faculty members, furious with Lee, wanted him kicked out of the program. While some thought the film showed promise, others saw it as overly ambitious and overbearing. They thought it lacked the technical skill, as well as the subtleties of presentation, that they were trying to teach. They were

*While at New York University Lee made a controversial
student film,* The Answer, *to rebut the racism portrayed in
D.W. Griffith's* Birth of a Nation.

offended, too, by the brashness, even the overt offensiveness of its topic and tone. One of the faculty who evaluated the film, Roberta Hodes, said later, "I just think it offended everyone. I felt offended, too, I'm ashamed to say."[10] Another professor, Eleanor Hamerow, saw it this way: "In the first year, we're trying to teach them the basics, and certainly the idea was to execute exercises, make small films, but within limits. He was trying to solve a problem overnight—the social problem with the blacks and the whites. He undertook to fix the great filmmaker who made that movie, D.W. Griffith. He was going to teach him a lesson."[11] After the uproar died down, the faculty voted, and Lee was allowed to stay in the program. *The Answer*, no longer available for viewing, is best remembered as an early work that indicated, in content and intent, the direction the young filmmaker would take in the future.

At the end of his first year, and despite the controversy surrounding *The Answer*, Lee won an assistantship at NYU that paid his tuition, and in exchange he worked in the school's equipment department. During his last two years, Lee honed his craft and as a senior delivered a final project, *Joe's Bed-Stuy Barbershop: We Cut Heads*, that was widely praised. Set in a barbershop in Brooklyn's Bedford-Stuyvestant neighborhood, the film is a comic look at a numbers-running operation that features believable characters and a warm, humorous tone. The score was composed by Lee's father, Bill, the first of many he would contribute to his son's movies. The cinematographer was Lee's grad school friend Ernest Dickerson, who would also go on to work with Lee on several films. Lee's grandmother, ever his ardent supporter, gave him some of the money to make the film, and she is listed as the movie's producer. *Joe's Bed-Stuy Barbershop* was shot in Brooklyn, using homes and storefronts belonging to family friends and starring an old friend from Morehouse, Monty Ross, in the leading role.

The faculty who had been so critical of *The Answer* lavished praise on Lee's senior project. Roberta Hodes recalls that "it was so alive and had such real characters."[12] It won Lee a Student Academy Award and was selected as the first student production shown at New York's Lincoln Center New Directors and New Film series.

Out into the Working World—and More Controversy

Lee graduated from NYU with his master's degree in film in 1982. He had signed with two talent agencies to find work in film, but after several months nothing had come through. Instead, he started working for a movie distribution company, where he cleaned and shipped movies. Still full of ideas and ambition, he started working on a new film idea he called *The Messenger,* about a young bicycle messenger in New York. Lee immediately ran into problems with financing and other realities of the working world. He met actor Lawrence Fishburne, who agreed to star in the film, but told Lee he would have to pay him and all other Screen Actors Guild (SAG) members SAG rates. Lee could not afford those rates, so he tried to make the film with unknown actors. He had applied for financing as an independent filmmaker and had won a grant from the American Film Institute. But SAG was able to block Lee's initiative, claiming his planned film was "too commercial" and therefore not able to qualify as an "independent" film that provided a waiver to allow nonunion actors.

Lee was furious and claimed that SAG's actions were racist. "I got a list of 10 films that had been given a waiver with the [previous] year," he later wrote. "All of them were done by white independent filmmakers. All of them worked with a whole lot more money than I had. Yet they said my film was too commercial. . . . That was a definite case of racism." He refused to give up. "I saw I made the classic mistakes of a young filmmaker, to be overly ambitious, do something beyond my means and capabilities. Going through the fire just made me more hungry, more determined that I couldn't fail again."[13] Lee eventually abandoned *The Messenger* over funding and labor issues and soon began work on a new project.

She's Gotta Have It

Lee's next project would be the one that finally got him noticed. Made on a shoestring budget and in just twelve days, *She's Gotta*

Choosing a Career

After realizing that he would never be a professional ballplayer, Spike Lee spent his late high school and early college years looking for what he really wanted to do. Morehouse College helped shape that. One of the finest traditional black colleges in the United States, it emphasizes teaching the history of African American achievement to its students.

At Morehouse, Lee attended plays and many movies, which he discussed in detail with friends, especially Monty Ross, who was an early collaborator. The two made a forgettable twenty-minute movie together, but it was enough to push Lee to write another screenplay, called *It's Homecoming*, which became the basis for his second movie, *School Daze*. The experience showed him the way to his career.

"I decided I wanted to be a filmmaker between my sophomore and junior years at Morehouse. Before I left for the summer of 1977, my advisor told me I really had to declare a major when I came back, because I'd used all my electives in my first two years." That's when Lee went home and picked up his Super-8 camera and "just started to shoot stuff." The time was right. "When school started again in September 1977, I declared my major in mass communications."

"A lot of things have happened to me in my life. Some higher being looked over me—pushed me in another direction, from the place I wanted to go to where I needed to go. It was just the right time for a young African-American filmmaker to break through. Fate has played a big part in my career, but you must also add talent, hard work, luck and timing. All those things contributed to my success."

Spike Lee: That's My Story and I'm Sticking To It, as told to Kaleem Aftab. New York: Norton, 2006, pp. 7, 14, 15.

Have It was written, produced, directed, and edited by Lee, and he had a costarring role, too. It is a humorous yet realistic portrayal of an African American woman and her romantic relationships, as well as a sly look at the double standard that applies to women and gender roles. The film starred Tracy

Camilla Johns as Nola Darling, a young black woman living in New York who has three boyfriends. One, played by Lee, was the character of Mars Blackmon, who would reappear in a later Lee film.

In *She's Gotta Have It*, Nola enjoys having three men in her life, and she does not want to conform to society's expectations that she choose only one. But the comic movie takes on a serious tone when one of the men sexually assaults her; in the film's conclusion, she leaves all three of the men.

She's Gotta Have It opened in San Francisco in 1986 and quickly found a distributor. When it opened in New York, the lines formed around the block. Lee claims this was a gimmick because he restricted the release to just one theater, which drove viewer interest and created the long lines. "Every night was sold out," he recalls. "And I would get there and hand out buttons. Me and my friends were selling *She's Gotta Have It* T-shirts." Lee had a shrewd grasp of marketing, and it showed. "From very early on—not that I was that sophisticated, but, coming from the independent world, I knew that millions and millions of dollars were not going to be spent on the promotion and marketing of my film. So in a lot of ways I had to market myself and market the brand of Spike Lee."[14]

That year at the Cannes Film Festival in France *She's Gotta Have It* won the Prix de la Jeunesse (Youth Prize), an important prize for a young filmmaker. The small indie film that cost Lee a total of $175,000 was a success and went on to make $8 million worldwide. It won praise for its cinematography, too, which had been done by Lee's frequent collaborator and NYU classmate Ernest Dickerson. Critics praised his evocative use of black and white photography, as well as the transformation to vivid color in the musical scenes. Reviewers also liked Lee's performance, which surprised him. "I never wanted to act," he claims. "The only reason I was in *She's Gotta Have It* is that we couldn't afford to pay anyone else."[15]

Yet, as with nearly every film he has done, it was also controversial. Some white critics claimed that it did not portray African American characters in a believable way, which Lee largely dismissed. Some black critics, especially female critics,

In 1986 Lee won the Cannes Film Festival's Prix de la Jeunesse award for his film She's Gotta Have It.

objected to the characterization of Nola, which they found sexist. But the majority of reviewers praised the film, some even calling Lee the "black Woody Allen," a reference to the New York director of such classics as *Annie Hall* and *Manhattan,* many of them focusing on New York and modern relationships. Lee did not care much for the comparison. He thought it was a simplistic response: two New Yorkers, writing films about relationships in the city. He thought it was laziness on the part of critics and that they ignored a main purpose of the film: to create a black sex comedy, offering a new perspective on African American relationships. With his next film, Lee continued to follow his own vision, in his own way, setting himself apart from anyone else.

School Daze

Fulfilling Lee's vision was his next film, *School Daze*, which came out in 1988. Set during homecoming at a fictionalized historical black college largely based on Morehouse, it is a musical comedy that seriously looks at the way African Americans discriminate against one another based on the lightness of their skin tone. Lee exposes how a social caste system exists in the black community, with light-skinned African Americans favored over darker-skinned blacks in careers, in love, and in life. Lee shot much of the film at Morehouse, but when the administration found out about the movie's content, they asked him to film elsewhere, and he moved shooting to Atlanta University. The film received both positive and negative reviews and was a financial success, bringing in $15 million. And once again Lee was a figure of controversy, especially in the black community, for some found the film to promote a negative view of African American life, and some believed it perpetuated stereotypes.

The same year he was making *School Daze,* Lee became a well-known face on American television, not through his films, but rather through a series of highly successful and entertaining ads he directed for Nike athletic shoes. Featuring superstar basketball player Michael Jordan and Lee in the character of Mars Blackmon, the commercials helped make Nike's Air Jordan shoes an international success and gained Lee an international audience. "There was a time when more people knew me as that crazy guy in those Nike commercials than knew I was Spike Lee, the director,"[16] he recalls.

School Daze (1988), a musical comedy partially shot at Morehouse College, dealt with skin tone issues within the black community.

While establishing his film and advertising career, Lee also formed his own production company, 40 Acres and a Mule. The name refers to the promise made to freed slaves by the U.S. government at the end of the Civil War to provide them with assets to begin their lives of freedom. The lands, confiscated from plantation owners, never made it into the hands of the freed blacks. Instead, the land reverted to most of the former slave owners and resulted in the share-cropper system of agriculture that provided lives of grinding poverty to generations of blacks. The phrase "40 acres and a mule" became a symbol of promises made, and broken, between whites and blacks.

It is a symbol, too, for the purpose of almost all of Lee's work: to offer an African American perspective on America today, especially on relations between whites and blacks. It was the focus of his next, and what many consider to be his finest, work, *Do the Right Thing*, a pivotal piece of filmmaking for Lee, and for American cinema.

Chapter 2

Do the Right Thing

In 1989 Spike Lee released *Do the Right Thing*, a work in which he played multiple roles: writer, director, producer, and actor. It is considered by many to be his best film and is also his most critically acclaimed and controversial movie, a work that would define him for the next two decades. Exploring the intersection of race, politics, and personal relationships, its genesis was an infamous event that took place in New York.

Howard Beach

The film was inspired in part by a notorious incident in Howard Beach, a neighborhood in the New York borough of Queens. On December 20, 1986, three black men went into a pizzeria in an Italian section of Howard Beach to use the phone. They were chased out of the pizzeria and through a predominantly white neighborhood by an angry gang of young Italian Americans, who then beat them with baseball bats. One of the African Americans, Michael Griffith, was chased onto a busy highway, where he was struck by a car and killed. The incident increased racial tension in New York, and a protest, led by the Reverend Al Sharpton, was held a week after the incident. Nine people were eventually convicted of criminal charges in the attack, and it remained a volatile symbol of the explosive nature of race relations in Queens and around the country.

"I wanted to do something to address [Howard Beach] and racism," said Lee about *Do the Right Thing*. "We took four things

Community and black leaders hold a vigil outside the New Park Pizza parlor in response to racial tensions in 1986. The incident inspired Lee's Do the Right Thing.

from it: the baseball bat, a black man gets killed, the pizzeria, and the conflict between blacks and Italian-Americans."[17] But what he did with that premise, and the complex way he presented his story, has resonated through the culture for decades.

Do the Right Thing is set on a block in the Bedford-Stuyvesant neighborhood of Brooklyn. The action takes place within twenty-four hours, on the hottest day of the year. The main character, Mookie (played by Lee), delivers pizza for Sal (Danny Aiello), the Italian American owner of Sal's Famous, one of the few white-owned businesses left in the neighborhood. Sal's sons, Vito (Richard Edson) and Pino (John Turturro), work with their father in the restaurant.

The neighborhood is home to a wide variety of characters. Mookie's sister, Jade (played by Lee's sister, Joie Lee), lives with him and is always telling him to grow up and be a man. His girlfriend, Tina (Rosie Perez), is raising their child in an apartment nearby. Da Mayor (Ossie Davis), a kindly drunk, talks to everyone and has a special affection for Mother Sister (Ruby

Dee), who watches over the neighborhood from her front stoop. Music comes from the radio station WE-LOVE, courtesy of D.J. Mister Señor Love Daddy (Samuel L. Jackson). And music also flows from the boom box of Radio Raheem (Bill Nunn), who plays "Fight the Power" by Public Enemy over and over.

Most of the kids in the neighborhood have grown up eating Sal's pizza, and it serves as a meeting place for them. Jade stops in for a slice, and it is obvious that Sal has a deep affection for her. When Buggin Out (Giancarlo Esposito), the local activist, enters the restaurant, he's angry. Why does Sal have pictures of Italian American stars like Frank Sinatra and Sylvester Stallone on his wall and no African Americans? Sal tells him, "When you open your own pizzeria, then you can put whoever you want on the wall."

Buggin Out takes his message to the streets, trying to get the neighborhood blacks to boycott Sal's, but the locals ignore him. Then Radio Raheem, his boom box blaring, enters Sal's, and Sal tells him to turn the music down. Radio refuses, and they begin to argue. According to Lee, he wanted the "temperature," of the

*For **Do The Right Thing** Lee played multiple roles including pizza delivery boy Mookie who works for an Italian American.*

neighborhood and his characters to keep rising, to show several points where things could either escalate or calm down. But tempers and temperatures just get hotter and hotter.

"I didn't want people to see the plot, but it's there. The most important thing is for people to see how big a part the heat plays in all of this. The heat tests everybody's patience, and it builds from small incidents: if Radio Raheem had turned down his radio, nothing would have happened. If Sal had put up a black person's picture on his Wall of Fame, there wouldn't have been any static. But it all culminates in a tragedy."[18]

From the spark of an argument comes the fire of a riot. Sal takes a baseball bat to Radio's boom box, and a fight breaks out. The police, all white, arrive, supposedly to calm things down. One officer gets Radio in a choke hold and suffocates him. Mookie, furious with Sal and about the death of his friend, picks up a trash can and hurls it through the window of the pizzeria. The crowd turns into a mob and begins to riot. Sal's Famous goes up in flames.

The final scene takes place the next morning as Sal sits in the smoldering remains of his restaurant, and Mookie comes by to get paid. Sal throws five hundred dollars in cash at him, spitting out his fury, unable to comprehend what happened or why. Mookie takes his money and walks home.

As the film ends, two quotes come up on the screen, one from Martin Luther King Jr. and one from Malcolm X:

King: "Violence as a way of achieving racial justice is both impractical and immoral. It is a descending spiral ending in destruction for all. The old law of an eye for an eye leaves everybody blind. It is immoral because it seeks to humiliate the opponent rather than win his understanding: it seeks to annihilate rather than convert. Violence is immoral because it thrives on hatred rather than love. It destroys community and makes brotherhood impossible. It leaves society in monologue rather than dialogue. Violence ends up defeating itself. It creates bitterness in the survivors and brutality in the destroyers."

Malcolm X: "I think there are plenty of good people in America, but there are also plenty of bad people in America and the bad ones are the ones who seem to have all the power and

The Studio's Point of View

Even before *Do the Right Thing* was made, the film was courting controversy. Spike Lee thought he had an agreement with the Hollywood giant Paramount Studios to produce the film, but they balked at signing, asking Lee to change the ending before they would agree to finance the movie.

"At the last moment, Paramount asked me to change the ending. They wanted Mookie and Sal to hug and be friends and sing 'We Are the World,'" Lee recalled. Lee refused to make the changes and decided to offer the film to other studios, eventually signing with Universal to make the picture.

"How I Made It: Spike Lee on *Do the Right Thing*," *New York*, April 7, 2008, p. 45.

Lee directs a scene in Do the Right Thing. *After he refused to change the film's ending for Paramount executives, Lee took the movie to Universal Studios.*

be in these positions to block things that you and I need. Because this is the situation, you and I have to preserve the right to do what is necessary to bring an end to that situation, and it doesn't mean that I advocate violence, but at the same time I am not against using violence in self-defense. I don't even call it violence when it's self-defense, I call it intelligence."[19]

A Heated Response

The response to *Do the Right Thing* was immediate, and visceral. Some critics, including David Denby and Joe Klein of *New York* magazine, thought Lee was trying to incite African Americans to riot. The *New York Times* put together a panel of writers and politicians to discuss the film. Political leaders, too, feared a violent backlash from the black community.

Mookie and pizza parlor owner Sal, played by Danny Aiello, discuss race in Do the Right Thing. *The film received praise and condemnation for its depiction of racial issues.*

Critics and the Fear of Riots

Some New York leaders, including the editorial staff of the *New York Times*, as well as *New York* magazine political columnist Joe Klein and *New York* film critic David Denby, thought *Do the Right Thing* was going to cause a political backlash in the African American community of New York.

"Joe Klein and David Denby felt that this film was going to cause riots," Lee recalled. "Young black males were going to emulate Mookie and throw garbage cans through windows. Like, 'How dare you release this film in summertime: *you know how they get in summertime, this is like playing with fire.*'" Lee was furious and called his critics racist. His attitude has mellowed over time. "I hold no grudges against them," he said recently. "But that was 20 years ago and it speaks for itself."

"How I Made It: Spike Lee on *Do the Right Thing*," *New York*, April 7, 2008, p. 45.

Lee completely rejected that interpretation. In a *New York Times* interview from 1989, he said, "For many white people, there is a view that black people have the vote and they can live next door to us and it's all done with and there's no more racism. As far as I'm concerned, racism is the most pressing problem in the United States; and I wanted the film to bring the issue into the forefront where it belongs. . . . I definitely don't have the answers for racism; but I feel that in order to get to the answers, we have to look at the issues of race and conflict and to say things are not all right."[20]

Lee's conclusion, in particular, seemed ambiguous and unsettling for critics. Lee did not understand that. In the wake of Howard Beach and other incidents of police violence against blacks the meaning for him was clear. "Black America is tired of having their brothers and sisters murdered by the police for no reason other than being black. I'm not advocating violence. I'm saying I can understand it. If the people are frustrated and feel oppressed and feel this is the only way they can act, I understand."[21]

Just How Realistic Is Lee's Depiction?

In addition to the controversies generated by the film's volatile topic, Lee was criticized for his depiction of the Bedford-Stuyvesant neighborhood. In 1988, when he filmed the movie, the area was notorious for its drug and criminal culture. Lee hired a crew to overhaul the one-block area he chose as his setting before he began shooting. They cleaned up a street littered with crack houses and painted and spruced up the exteriors prior to filming. There was no mention of drugs in the movie at all, and that, too, raised concerns about Lee's objectivity in depicting the film's setting.

The criticism rankled him. "This film is not about drugs," he claimed. He turned the criticism back on the critics, claiming, "Drugs is in every level of society today in America. How many of you journalists saw *Working Girl* or *Rain Man* and questioned, where are the drugs? Nobody!"[22]

The film also sparked a long feud between Lee and African American cultural critic Stanley Crouch. In an article in the *Village Voice* titled "Do the Race Thing: Spike Lee's Afro-Fascist Chic," Crouch claimed that Lee was little more than a promoter of black nationalism. "The fact that Spike Lee is a talented guy is inarguable," said Crouch. "But if you make movies as consistently inferior to the movies of a man like Woody Allen or Martin Scorsese and cry 'racism' or imply racism, when your movies are not as successful as theirs are—what is that? On a human level, his comprehension of other people is far more shallow than theirs is, and that's the basic problem that he's had from the beginning of his career, the fundamental shallowness that you get from a propagandist."[23]

Praise for the Writing and Acting

Not all of the critical response to the film was negative. Many critics found *Do the Right Thing* to be the most thoughtful, insightful look at race relations to appear in years. *New York Times* critic Vincent Canby said, "In all of the earnest, solemn, humorless discussions about the social and political implications of Spike Lee's *Do the Right Thing*, an essential fact tends to be overlooked: it is one terrific movie . . . living, breathing, riveting proof of the arrival of an abundantly gifted new talent."[24] Roger Ebert of the *Chicago Sun-Times* thought Lee "had done an almost impossible thing. He'd made a movie about race in America that empathized with all the participants. He didn't draw lines or take sides but simply looked with sadness at one racial flashpoint that stood for many others."[25]

Do the Right Thing won Lee nearly universal praise for its script and for the superb ensemble acting. Canby noted that "the telling of all this is so buoyant, so fresh, so exact, and so moving that one comes out of the theater elated by the display of sheer cinematic wizardry." Many praised the characters as alive and believable, vividly brought to life by fine acting performances. Lee had cast Ossie Davis and Ruby Dee, famous African American actors of stage and screen, in the roles of the "elders" of the community. They witness the action of the film, as an ordinary day turns extraordinary, and their neighborhood is destroyed in a torrent of violence with tragic proportions.

Critics also praised Danny Aiello's portrayal of Sal. He, too, is a fully realized, believable character, not a stereotypical racist. For many, Sal was not portrayed as an evil, one-sided bigot, but rather as a complex, well-developed character. Aiello's portrayal of him as a man who loses his temper, then loses everything, is, for many, one of the film's highlights. Lee's representation of Mookie received warm accolades, too, as a character who, in just twenty-four hours, has his eyes opened and his life changed.

Ernest Dickerson's cinematography also received special praise. The movie has a riveting look, from the first scenes featuring Rosie Perez dancing to Public Enemy's "Fight the Power," to the closing frames, as Mookie walks down the somber street of his neighborhood the morning after the cataclysmic riot that changes all their lives. The riot scenes are realistic and terrifying, as two members of the cast, Joie Lee and Richard Edson, recalled: "You'd stop and see the pizza parlor burning, 200 extras running out in the street, and you'd think, 'This could be the real thing." Edson, who played Sal's son Vito, said further, "The question is, why do these things keep happening? Who's gonna do the right thing? Would I? And what is the right thing, at the moment of truth?"[26]

Critics also praised the movie's music, noting how its intensity parallels the action. Lee's father, Bill Lee, composed the score, and the soundtrack also includes the work of many prominent African American musicians, including Public Enemy, Ruben Blades, Take 6, Al Jarreau, and Gerald Alston. Many commentators noted how Lee's use of "Fight the Power" is particularly effective, framing the film from its opening credits to its violent climax.

The Awards Season, and More Controversy

In the spring of 1989, *Do the Right Thing* was shown at the Cannes Film Festival, the site of Lee's previous triumph with *She's Gotta Have It*. But this time his new movie went up against the first work of another young filmmaker, Stephen Soderbergh, who had entered *sex, lies, and videotape*. When Soderbergh won, his first response was shock: He was sure that the honor should have gone to *Do the Right Thing*. Lee agreed. "We were robbed. Ten films received awards and we didn't get one. I feel we entered the best of the festival." He had particular scorn for German filmmaker and Cannes judge Wim Wenders. "I heard that Wenders said that Mookie wasn't enough of a hero," he said. Lee accused Wenders of not understanding the movie's pivotal moment, when Mookie throws the trash can through Sal's window, and of not being able to separate Mookie from his creator, Spike Lee. "I think they saw Spike Lee throwing that trash can through the window."[27]

Lee did win several awards for *Do the Right Thing*, including the L.A. Film Critics Awards for best picture, director, and screenplay. When the Academy Award nominations for 1989 were announced, Lee had been nominated for best screenplay, and Danny Aiello for best supporting actor, but the film never

Spike with some of the cast of Do the Right Thing. *Pictured at the Cannes Film Festival in 1989, from left to right, are Richard Edson, Spike's sister Joie Lee, Spike Lee, Ossie Davis, and Ruby Dee. The film was nominated for best screenplay and best supporting actor.*

made it into the more prestigious categories of Best Film or Best Director, a fact that Lee termed racist. At the Oscars in 1989, actress Kim Basinger, introducing a clip of *Dead Poets Society*, nominated in the best film category, departed from her script to tell the audience that *Do the Right Thing* had not been nominated, even though it was clearly, in her opinion, the best film of the year. Neither Lee nor Aiello won that year, but the film's importance had been firmly established.

A Political Point of View

In addition to his treatment of the politics of racism, Lee had another motive in mind when he made the film: He wanted New York City mayor Ed Koch out of office. He blamed Koch, who was mayor from 1978 to 1989, for creating the bitter racial divide that separated New Yorkers during the era; Howard Beach and other incidents had happened during his administration. "Anytime you hear Ed Koch talk about 'savages' and 'animals,' you know he's talking about young black males,"[28] Lee claimed.

The film was released in the summer, just before the mayoral elections in New York, and in the movie, there is graffiti stating "Dump Koch" on walls. At the end, while the smoke is fading away, Mister Señor Love Daddy is encouraging his listeners to "Go out and vote!" Whether or not Lee influenced anyone's opinion is not known, but Koch went down to defeat in 1989, and New York City's first black mayor, David Dinkins, was elected.

Do the Right Thing in Retrospect

In 2008, as the twentieth anniversary of the release of *Do the Right Thing* approached, critical commentary continued to focus on how pivotal the film was, both to American cinema and to

Members of the Do The Right Thing *cast get together in New York City in 2009 for a twentieth anniversary screening of the film. The film remains relevant today, even after twenty years.*

Lee's career. Writing in the *New Yorker*, Richard Brody described the nature of Lee's achievement. "*Do the Right Thing* has lost none of its strength. . . . If it exposes Lee's limitations as a director—his lack of perspective resulting from his attachment to, and advocacy for, the community that he films—it also reflects the unique sensibility that, to this day, gives his films the immediacy of a news report from the front lines of the city. Lee's originality, as well as his modernism, lies in his translation of the free-form poetry of popular speech into script, performance, and images."[29]

Do the Right Thing also dominated the reception of Lee's later work, especially as he continued to explore the intersection of race, politics, and personal relationships in his next films, *Mo' Better Blues, Jungle Fever,* and *Malcolm X.*

Chapter 3

Race, Politics, and Personal Relationships

Spike Lee's next three films were *Mo' Better Blues, Jungle Fever,* and *Malcolm X,* and in each of these movies, Lee continued to explore African American life, particularly the intersection of race, politics, and personal relationships. *Mo' Better Blues* reflected Lee's exploration of a life devoted to an African American musical expression, jazz. *Jungle Fever* took on the volatile topic of an interracial affair and its consequences to a family and a community. *Malcolm X* was the realization of a lifelong dream of Lee's: to provide a portrait of one of the pivotal figures of twentieth-century America—the controversial, charismatic Black Muslim civil rights leader. Though each of them sparked controversy, they were also evidence of the growth and breadth of Lee's artistic vision.

Mo' Better Blues

In *Mo' Better Blues,* released in 1990, Lee again played four roles: screenwriter, director, producer, and actor. He was inspired to make the film to pay homage to jazz, an African American musical tradition he grew up with and whose inspiration and history he wanted to share with a new generation. "Jazz is an art form we created. And, very sadly, it's musicians like Wynton and Branford Marsalis, and Terence Blanchard and the older cats who are trying to save this tradition, which a lot of young black kids—not all of them—aren't hearing; so the black community loses some of its tradition."[30] The film did in part represent a change in themes for Lee, centering on the life of a black jazz trumpeter, Bleek Gilliam, but focusing on the personal relationships, not the racial conflicts, of Bleek's life. "*Mo' Better Blues* is about relationships," Lee said. "It's not about man-woman relationships, but about relationships in general—Bleek's relationship to his father and manager, and his relationship to two female friends. Bleek's true love is music, and he is trying to find the right balance."[31]

The movie is set in Brooklyn, and the opening scene shows Bleek as a young boy practicing his horn as his friends gather outside, urging him to come out and play. Bleek's mother insists, loud and long, that he stay home and practice; his father, too, urges him to play, but with a greater gentleness. As Bleek plays his scale studies, the scene moves to the present, where we see Bleek performing at a jazz club with his group.

Bleek (played by Denzel Washington) plays with skill and confidence to an appreciative crowd. Shadow Henderson (Wesley Snipes), a showy saxophonist in Bleek's band, takes a solo as Bleek

In Mo' Better Blues, Lee directed Denzel Washington in a story of a young black musician whose life story inspired Lee to make the movie.

leaves the stage. He meets his manager, Giant (Lee), in the wings. This is Bleek's world, where he is successful, but something's missing. We learn that he has two girlfriends, the lovely, seductive Clarke (Cynda Williams), and the more serious, less glamorous Indigo (Joie Lee). He loves them both but cannot choose between them, as much as they want him to. His dedication to his art is in question as well.

The story revolves around Bleek's search for balance in his life. He loves his music, and it is the center of his life. Where can he find the time, and place, for love? When his world falls apart, who can he turn to for comfort, for direction, for meaning in his life?

Mo' Better Blues was, in part, Lee's tribute to his father, Bill Lee, a jazz musician, and the composer of the film's score. The movie is framed by scenes of father and son, the first with Bleek and his dad, the last with Bleek and his own son. One of the movie's themes is responsibility—as a man, a musician, and a friend. Lee wanted to be clear about one crucial point: that Bleek was not the clichéd black jazzman addicted to drugs or alcohol. Instead, the focus was on a man and his relationships with his art and the people around him.

Critical Indifference

Mo'Better Blues did not do very well at the box office, and the critical response was indifferent. Coming after *Do the Right Thing,* the film was strikingly different in tone and purpose, and most critics dismissed it as a poor effort. "Spike Lee is an exhilarating mix of brilliance and bravado, of artist, businessman, and preacher," wrote Caryn James in the *New York Times.* "A new Spike Lee film might be anything at all except dull and conventional, or at least that seemed true until *Mo' Better Blues.* From characters to camera angles, this story of a self-absorbed jazz trumpeter is one long cliché, the kind that might make his most loyal admirers wince and wonder, 'Spike, what happened?'"[32]

Other critics, including Roger Ebert, thought the film was flawed, but still had spirit. "It's a less passionate and angry film than . . . *Do the Right Thing,* and less inspired, too," Ebert wrote.

Lee directs cast and crew during a shoot for Mo' Better Blues. Critics' response was mixed, and the film did not do well at the box office.

"It suffers a little from the 'second-novel syndrome,' the pressure on an artist to follow up a great triumph. But it's a logical film to come at this point in Lee's career, since it's about the time and career pressures on a young artist." The movie, Ebert concludes, "is not a great film, but an interesting one, which is almost as rare."[33]

Accused of Anti-Semitism

The film also sparked controversy, not for Lee's treatment of racial conflict, but over his depiction of two Jewish characters. Bleek's group plays at a club owned by two Jewish brothers, Moe and Josh Flatbush (John and Nicholas Turturro), who are portrayed as greedy, manipulative men who take advantage of the black jazz musicians. "What could have been going through Spike Lee's mind when he invented the Jewish club owners . . . money-grubbing, devious, ugly stereotypes with sharks' smiles?"[34] wrote James in her review in the *New York Times*.

Lee was stung by the criticism. On the advice of his lawyer, he wrote an op-ed piece for the *New York Times* in which he defended himself against accusations of anti-Semitism. In his characteristic confrontational style, Lee declared, "I challenge anyone to tell me why I can't portray two club owners who happen to be Jewish and who exploit the black jazz musicians who work for them. All Jewish club owners are not like this, but these two are."[35]

Lee did not let the criticism of *Mo' Better Blues* deter him in any way. As always, he followed his own muse. In his next film, 1991's *Jungle Fever,* he returned to a more familiar theme: racial politics in America. This time, the focus was interracial romance, and he examines the way that race, ethnicity, and skin tone dictate choices, and even happiness, in personal relationships.

Jungle Fever

In *Jungle Fever*, Lee returned to the provocative issue of race in the story of a romance between a black man and a white woman. The movie, written, directed, and produced by Lee, tells the story of the interracial affair between Flipper Purify (played by Wesley Snipes), a successful African American architect, and his Italian American secretary, Angie Tucci (Annabella Sciorra). When the film begins, Flipper is a happily married man, with a wife, a child, and a beautiful home in Harlem. He needs a secretary and asks the office boss for an African American. Instead, he gets Angie, from the Italian neighborhood of Bensonhurst. They learn to work together and spend long hours in the office.

When Flipper and Angie begin to develop strong feelings for each other they hurdle headlong into an affair, with disastrous consequences. Flipper tells his best friend, Cyrus (played by Lee), who is furious, especially because Flipper's lover is white. When Flipper's wife finds out, she kicks him out of the house; she, too, is stung by his betrayal, and especially because he has chosen a white woman over her. When Angie's father finds out about Flipper, he beats her. Angie's fiancé, Paulie (John Turturro), faces scorn and contempt from his own Italian American friends and family, who also see her betrayal as more hurtful because she has chosen a black man.

In one of the film's finest scenes, Flipper's wife, Drew, talks about his infidelity with her girlfriends. What ensues is an emotional discussion about race. They discuss how the lightness or darkness of a black person's skin determines personal relationships and a harmful social hierarchy in the African American community, echoing back to a similar theme in *School Daze*. Drew is half-white; she always thought that Flipper might have married her because of the lighter tone of her skin; now she's losing him to someone even "lighter." In a parallel scene, Paulie's Italian American friends discuss Angie's betrayal and how some of them have skin so dark they have been rejected by white women, making them cling to their whiteness as a way of clinging to their identity.

Flipper and Angie move in together, but the relationship does not last. Lee shows how the two of them are drawn together because of their illusions about each other: The "jungle fever" they

Lee directs Wesley Snipes, left and Annabella Sciorra, right, in 1991's Jungle Fever.

suffer from is based on what Lee calls "sexual myths." "When you're a black person in this country, you're constantly bombarded with the myth of the white woman as the epitome of beauty," he said. Similarly, Angie "bought into the myth that the black male is a stud." Further, Lee wanted to show how all the characters are trying to find out who they really are. "The people in the film are constantly talking about their identity, where they belong."[36]

Gator: Portrait of a Drug Addict

Jungle Fever also includes Lee's first treatment of drugs in the black community. He had been criticized for not presenting the corrosive effects of drugs in *Do the Right Thing,* and he felt *Jungle Fever* offered him the opportunity to present the issue. Flipper's brother Gator, played with searing intensity by Samuel L. Jackson, is a crack addict. His addiction has torn his family apart, including his parents, the Good Reverend Doctor Purify (Ossie Davis) and Lucinda Purify (Ruby Dee). Gator has repeatedly taken money from them, stolen from them, and refused their help. In one of the movie's most harrowing moments, Flipper goes to a crack house to find Gator, to try one last time to rescue his brother. But Gator is past saving, and in the end, is shot and killed by his own father.

Lee says he based the relationship of Gator and the Reverend on that of rhythm-and-blues singer Marvin Gaye, a drug addict who was shot and killed by his father. Lee also wanted to show why a character like Gator had fallen so low and "how crack is totally wiping out generations of African-Americans."[37]

Critical response to *Jungle Fever* was largely positive, and the film did well at the box office, taking in about $33 million. Commentators praised Lee's powerful, provocative treatment of what Desson Howe of the *Washington Post* called "a politically charged situation, [stirred] up with color, music, and irony." Yet for Howe and many critics, the relationship between Flipper and Angie was not well developed or believable. "Lee's so interested in the ripple effect they cause, he almost forgets the affair itself,"[38] Howe wrote. Still, audiences and commentators alike were drawn to the film's brutal honesty, "the fearless discussion

In Jungle Fever, Samuel L. Jackson portrays Gator, a drug addict. The character allowed Lee to explore addiction's effect on a family.

of things both races would rather not face,"[39] as Roger Ebert said in the *Chicago Sun-Times.*

Once again, the film's cinematography and score won wide praise. "As always, Lee's visual purposes are beautifully realized—or kaleidoscoped—by the inimitable cinematographer Ernest Dickerson," wrote Desson Howe. "The movie is delirious with good music, including Terence Blanchard's memorable, jazzy-symphonic score and 12—count 'em, 12—songs from Stevie Wonder."[40]

Factual and Autobiographical Elements

Lee has discussed the origins for *Jungle Fever*'s story, drawn from the headlines and his own family experience. The film is dedicated to Yusef Hawkins, a young African American who was murdered in 1989 in the Italian American neighborhood of Bensonhurst in New York. "One day he wanted to check out a used car and ventured into a neighborhood, which happened to be a predominantly Italian-American neighborhood, and he was shot,"[41] says Lee. Hawkins's death became another symbol, for Lee and other members of the black community, of the racial hatred that still exists and erupts into violence against African Americans in Bensonhurst and around the country.

On another, more personal, level, the film echoes Lee's own family's experience. Just a year after his mother died in 1977, Lee's father, Bill, married a white woman, Susan Kaplan, causing a rift in Lee's relationship with his father that has never healed. When *Jungle Fever* came out, Lee described their relationship. "We don't get along, but it's not because she's white. I was my mother's first child, so my stepmother's never going to be my mother."[42] Yet, though Lee insisted that his father's remarriage did not influence the making of the film, Bill Lee had a different take. "That's directly talking about me and my wife in a negative way,"[43] he told *Jet* magazine. The movie put another strain on their relationship, which continued to deteriorate over the next several years.

With his reputation for controversy and pointed questions about race and politics firmly in mind, Lee went on to his next project. It was his biggest, most ambitious film to date, and the realization of a dream nurtured since film school: a biographical portrait of political and religious leader Malcolm X.

Malcolm X

Epic in scope and ambition, *Malcolm X*, released in 1992, was a movie that took Lee two full years to complete and was plagued with problems from the start. Over the course of those two years, Lee fought to direct the picture, lost studio backing and won new financing, and created a work that sparked controversy before and after its release. Though never as popular or financially successful as *Do the Right Thing*, *Malcolm X* is considered a monumental piece of filmmaking, the most ambitious film of one of the most ambitious filmmakers in the country.

The film is based on *The Autobiography of Malcolm X*, which was published after the political and religious leader's assassination in 1965. Lee read the book in middle school, and remembers that it "changed the way I thought, it changed the way I acted."[44] Making a movie version of Malcolm's life became a life-long dream: From the time Lee and Ernest Dickerson were in graduate school, they talked about a film adaptation of the book.

The film rights to the life of Malcolm X belonged to producer Marvin Worth and Warner Brothers, who initially had hired acclaimed director Norman Jewison, veteran of such racially sensitive movies as *In the Heat of the Night* and *A Soldier's Story*, to direct the movie. Jewison began working on a script in 1990 and had already hired Denzel Washington to play the lead when Lee made public his desire to direct the picture. Lee claimed that because Jewison was white, he could not do a credible job on the project. Jewison recalled that he felt that Lee "had pulled the race card, so I met with him."[45] Lee argued that Jewison did not have the "deep understanding of the black psyche" that he possessed. Jewison was furious and vented his feelings on a Canadian television show, claiming, "For an artist to say that another artist can't cope with a story because of skin color is ridiculous."[46] After meeting face to face with Lee and Worth, Jewison ultimately turned the project over to Lee, saying that he had done all he could on the film. Lee thanked the director, claiming, "He did not have to do that. It was his film."[47]

By that point, several different writers had developed scripts based on the *Autobiography*. Lee chose to base his version on a

Malcolm X

Malcolm X was born Malcolm Little in 1925 in Omaha, Nebraska. His father, Earl Little, was a minister and follower of the Black Nationalist Marcus Garvey, an association that brought danger to his family: The Ku Klux Klan drove the Little family from Omaha. They settled next in Lansing, Michigan, and again were the subjects of terror: Their home was burned to the ground by white racists, and Earl Little was found murdered. When Malcolm's mother, Louise, suffered a nervous breakdown, Malcolm and his siblings were put into foster homes.

Malcolm was an excellent student, but after years of facing racial prejudice, he dropped out of school and became involved in using and selling drugs. Arrested for robbery in 1946, he was sent to prison for ten years. There, his life was transformed. He began to study the teachings of the Nation of Islam, headed by Elijah Muhammad, who preached that blacks were superior to whites and that since white society kept blacks from economic and social equality, blacks should seek a separate nation of their own making. Converting to the faith, he renamed himself Malcolm X to express the fact that his ancestors' African name was unknown, while "Little" was a slave name inherited from his forebears' white masters. When he was released from prison in 1952, he moved to Chicago to work with Elijah Muhammad. Soon, he was the popular—and feared—face of the Nation of Islam, a fiery preacher who spoke to huge crowds of black people, drawing thousands to the faith and inspiring fear in many whites, including law enforcement officials, who feared his message of racial separatism and his claim that blacks must achieve their goals "by any means necessary."

He was at odds with other black religious and political leaders, too, including Martin Luther King Jr., whose goals of racial equality and integration he derided. But gradually, he changed his point of view. In 1964 he broke with the Nation of Islam and founded his own group, the Muslim Mosque. He went to Africa and the Middle East, making the Muslim pilgrimage to Mecca known as the hajj. The experience transformed him, and he returned to the United States committed to the fight for civil rights. But his new beliefs, especially his message of harmony, made him an enemy of the Nation of Islam. He began to receive death threats, and on February 21, 1965, he was assassinated while making a speech in New York. The three men arrested for his murder were members of the Nation of Islam.

screenplay originally written by famed African American author James Baldwin. But Lee also did a good deal of research, and rewriting, himself. With Denzel Washington, he reworked Baldwin's version. They took the project very seriously. They were creating a portrait of a renowned figure of the civil rights movement for a new generation of African Americans who might not be aware of his significance, and they knew they had to present it with clarity, nuance, and artistry. "We both knew a lot was riding on this film," Lee recalls. "We could not go anywhere without being reminded by black folks, . . . 'Don't mess this one up.'"[48]

Making the Movie

Lee had a clear vision of what he wanted to do in *Malcolm X*: to introduce the charismatic and controversial leader to a new generation of Americans. He wanted the black audience to "come out of the theater inspired and moved to do something positive." He also wanted to help redefine Malcolm X for the white

Denzel Washington's Malcolm X prays in a mosque during filming. Lee sought and received permission from the Saudi Arabian government to shoot scenes in Mecca.

The Meaning of Malcolm X Today

Malcolm X was a personal hero to Lee and to a generation of African Americans who learned of him through *The Autobiography of Malcolm X*, which was dictated to Alex Haley, later the acclaimed author of *Roots*, and published the year of his death, 1965. Lee was concerned that Malcolm's legacy not be forgotten. He wanted to create a film that outlined the man and his work so that he would be remembered and celebrated by current and future generations.

"I think the resurgence of Malcolm is about a void that young people are trying to fill. Ossie Davis said it best when he delivered the eulogy at Malcolm's funeral: 'He was our shining black prince, our manhood.' Young black men today need role models, and it's a shame we have to dig up a dead man instead of finding someone who walks among us."

Spike Lee, interviewed by James Verniere, *Sight and Sound*, February 1993, p. 10.

Malcolm X was an inspiration to a generation of African Americans.

audience "because for the most part, their view of Malcolm came from the white media, which portrayed him as anti-white, anti-Semitic, and pro-violence." He especially wanted to appeal to a young audience, and so he made his first PG-13 film. "We feel this is an important piece of American history and people, especially young kids, need to see this."[49]

Lee began to shoot *Malcolm X* in 1990. Right away, problems surfaced between Lee and the studio backing the film, Warner Brothers. The studio put up $20 million for a two-hour movie; Lee wanted $33 million for a movie he planned to be significantly longer. In his confrontational style, Lee complained about the "plantation" mentality at the studio, likening the studio heads to the "masters" overseeing slaves in the Old South. Warner Brothers also did not want to spend the money to send the crew to the Middle East and Africa to film key scenes from Malcolm's life or to finance the postproduction costs. So with a significant portion of the film left to complete, Lee made an appeal to several successful African Americans, including Bill Cosby, Oprah Winfrey, Magic Johnson, and Michael Jordan. They all contributed to funding the completion of the movie, which assured that it would fulfill Lee's vision.

To make the film as authentic as possible, Lee approached the government of Saudi Arabia to ask permission to shoot scenes of Malcolm X making the holy Muslim pilgrimage to Mecca known as the hajj. Although Lee and other non-Muslim crew members were not allowed into the country for filming, Muslim actors and technicians were allowed to film the key scenes. They became the first crew in history to film in Mecca.

Malcolm X, three and half hours in length, traces the life of the charismatic leader from his harrowing childhood, to his years as a street hoodlum, to his imprisonment and conversion to the Nation of Islam faith. From there, the movie charts his intellectual, spiritual, and political growth from a fiery Black Muslim preacher who believed in racial separatism to a man with a more moderate and nuanced approach to racial conflict and reconciliation. The final part of the film deals with his break with the Nation of Islam and its leader, Elijah Muhammad, and his travels to Egypt and Mecca in the final year of his life. The film ends with his return and his assassination by members of the Nation of Islam. In the epilogue, Ossie Davis reads the eulogy he actually gave for Malcolm at his funeral service in 1965.

Lee's Critics Respond

Even before the film was released, it had gained the notoriety often associated with Lee's films. Warner Brothers was so concerned about a possible violent reaction to the film in the black community that they prescreened it for police forces across the country. According to Lee, when the movie was shown to the police in Los Angeles, "the cops loved it." As with *Do the Right Thing,* he claimed critics had prejudged the film, determining that it would incite riots. "They were expecting a film that for three hours and twenty-one minutes would be saying. 'C'mon, black folks, let's get some guns and kill every white person in America,' but in the end the critics were saying, 'This film is *mild.*'"[50] Lee also came under fire from a group of African Americans, the United Front to Preserve the Memory of Malcolm X, which was headed by writer Amiri Baraka. They questioned Lee's treatment of the leader, as well as the presentation of his assassination at the hands of members of the Nation of Islam. In an open letter, Baraka listed their complaints: "Our distress about Spike's making a film on Malcolm is based on our analysis of the films he has already made, their caricature of Black people's lives, their dismissal of our struggle and the implication of their description of the Black nation as a few besieged Buppies [black, upwardly mobile professionals] surrounded by irresponsible repressive lumpen [displaced underclass people]."[51] Lee rejected Baraka's objections, claiming that "Malcolm X belongs to everybody," adding, "What bothered me about Baraka's argument was that he was saying that the reason why this film would not be good was that I was middle class. I think my first five films cover a lot of aspects of African-American society."[52]

Within the film community, critical response to *Malcolm X* was divided. While many critics praised the scope of Lee's vision in creating the film, some felt it lacked his former artistic passion. "Spike Lee has accomplished something historic in movies: a rousing, full-sized epic about a defiantly idealist black hero whose humanitarianism never extends to turning the other cheek,"[53] wrote *Rolling Stone* critic Peter Travers. Terrence Rafferty of the *New Yorker* disagreed: "The responses Lee aims for are the clear, pedagogically effective ones rather than the disturbing, irresolvable ones that Malcolm's own account evokes on almost every page [of the *Autobiography*]," he wrote. "The movie is disappointingly impersonal; it doesn't provide readers of the autobiography anything like a fresh vision of its remarkable subject. Lee assumes Malcolm's greatness and then simply illustrates it."[54]

Denzel Washington was widely praised for his interpretation of Malcolm X. Vincent Canby in the *New York Times* stated that he "does for *Malcolm X* what Ben Kingsley did for *Gandhi.*" In a note critiquing the acting and the writing of the film, Canby noted, "Mr. Washington not only looks the part, but he also has the psychological heft, the intelligence, and the reserve to give the film the dramatic excitement that isn't always apparent in the screenplay."[55] Washington garnered several Best Actor awards for his role. He also received an Academy Award nomination for Best Actor but did not win the Oscar.

The film made $48 million at the box office, and Lee also had success with a line of clothing he developed and marketed based on the film, as "X" caps became popular all over the country. It also brought a new audience to *The Autobiography of Malcolm X*, which reached the top of the bestseller lists nearly thirty years after it was published.

While the film did not garner major awards, it did establish Lee firmly as a major voice in filmmaking, able to handle a work of epic proportions. Weary after years of work on *Malcolm X* and ready for a change in tone and subject matter, Lee next chose to concentrate on smaller subjects, closer to his New York roots.

Chapter 4

A Change in Direction

The years 1993 to 2000 represented a change in direction for Spike Lee. He made films very different in character and tone from his earlier work and suffered a slump in critical circles and at the box office. His reaction was often bitter and caustic, and he also engaged in a rather public controversy with another major filmmaker. In addition, Lee made changes in his personal life, getting married and starting a family. And he wrote a book about his greatest avocational passion, basketball. It was a new era for the filmmaker.

Crooklyn

The film Lee made after *Malcolm X* could not have been more different, in content and intent. *Crooklyn*, released in 1994, is a heavily autobiographical work, developed out of a story idea created by Lee's sister, Joie. Joie and her brother Cinqué wrote the first draft of a story about a middle-class black family growing up in the 1970s in Brooklyn. They showed an early draft to Lee, hoping for a critique. "They came to me not to make the film, but to say, 'Do you know anybody who could help us get this made?'" Lee recalls. "I read it, and I said, 'I will make it.'"[56]

The movie depicts the life of the Carmichael family: a dad who is a jazz musician, a mom who is a teacher, and five feisty kids. The movie is set in the 1970s, featuring a group of middle-class black kids playing with their friends and enjoying the kind of carefree life in the streets of Brooklyn that has all but disappeared in the modern era. The ending is steeped in sadness as the children's beloved mother becomes ill and dies of cancer, and the final scenes show their uncomprehending grief.

Despite its clear autobiographical elements, Lee insisted that *Crooklyn* was a work of fiction. Delroy Lindo, who plays the father in the movie, suggested that Lee's stance "was an issue of Spike not being ready psychologically and emotionally to have his family history delved into."[57] Lee was going through a very difficult time with his father. During the filming of *Malcolm X*, Bill Lee was arrested for heroin possession. He tried to get off by telling the arresting officers that he was the son of Spike Lee. It was a moment of public and painful revelation for Lee and his siblings. They knew their father had become a heroin addict, and now the world knew. After the film's release, Bill asked Lee for a loan to pay bills. Lee refused, driving a further wedge between father and son. Yet the father in *Crooklyn* has none of Bill Lee's negative traits and is an idealized character. Some critics speculated that it was Lee's desire to promote a sentimental version of his childhood, rather than the reality of his

In 1994's Crooklyn Lee depicted the life of middle-class African Americans in Brooklyn during the 1970s.

life at the time, that prompted him to create such a positive portrait of a family, and of the father figure especially.

Crooklyn won muted praise from some critics, who used words like "romanticized," and "nostalgic" to describe its tone. Janet Maslin in the *New York Times* called it "so mild that it is the first Spike Lee film with the potential to be turned into a television show. More importantly, it is the first one to display real warmth of heart."[58] Lee responded with characteristic prickliness: "I just have to do the films I want to make. I do a film like this, they say it is too mild. I do *Do the Right Thing*, they accuse me of trying to incite 35 million Americans to burn down America."[59]

The film, which cost $14 million to make, barely made that much at the box office in the United States. This concerned Lee, because the money a movie makes often determines the financing possibilities for later films. Lee's next venture was more in keeping with his earlier work and had a distinguished background as well.

Clockers

Clockers, released in 1995, was a grim, realistic view of the havoc wreaked on the urban black community by crack cocaine. Based on the novel of the same name by Richard Price, the movie was originally supposed to be directed by the renowned director Martin Scorsese, who found himself too busy with other projects and asked Lee to take it on. Lee eagerly took over the project from someone he revered as a director and mentor. Scorsese had long been a supporter of Lee's, dating back to Lee's days as a graduate student at NYU.

Lee rewrote the screenplay, making key changes to the story. The original screenplay was a murder mystery focusing on police detective Rocco Klein and his investigation of a drug-related murder. Lee's rewrite centered on the character of Strike, the African American "clocker" of the title. A clocker is a member of the lowest class of drug dealer, someone who is available "round-the-clock" to deliver crack cocaine. In particular, Lee wanted to examine the conflict between Strike and his brother, the clean-living, hard-working Victor. Victor confesses

On His "Signature Shot"

Lee's signature shot, the one he's best known for, is the "dolly shot," which gives the effect of an actor floating along rather than walking. To achieve the effect, Lee mounts an actor on a dolly, and then moves the dolly and the camera simultaneously. He describes how he created it:

> The first time I used it was in *Mo' Better Blues* with my character Giant. To get that shot you have to lay dolly tracks. Then you put the camera on the dolly. Then you put the actors on the dolly also. Then you move the dolly along.

Lee's simple description of the shot belies its power. He has used it to great effect in most of his films, often to indicate an altered state of mind in a character. It is especially effective in the conclusion of *Malcolm X*, as the camera follows Denzel Washington as Malcolm, shooting up from the dolly into his face as he seems to float in the air, suspended in time, just before he enters the Audubon Ballroom, the site of his assassination. The scene is brief—just a few minutes—but it is powerful, suggesting that Malcolm knew how his fate would play out.

Erich Leon Harris, "The Demystification of Spike Lee," *MovieMaker*, March 1997, p. 127.

Lee always likes to put a "signature shot" in his movies.

to a murder that Klein suspects was committed by Strike; the film follows the investigation, exploring the dark, tragic world of crack cocaine and its victims.

Lee's cast included the celebrated actor Harvey Keitel as Klein, and Delroy Lindo as the drug lord who controls Strike. Lee cast an unknown actor from the Bronx, Mekhi Phifer, in the lead, in what would be a break-out performance, with Isaiah Washington as Victor.

The film's tough subject and somber tone may have led to its mixed critical response. While some praised it, others were less enthusiastic, and it did poorly at the box office, bringing in only $13 million.

Still rejecting anyone else's efforts to define him or his vision, Lee responded to the film's critics with characteristic vehemence. "White America, they just want black men to always be smiling. So if you don't do that all the time, then they label you the Angry Black Man. As if we had nothing to be angry about, anyway! I mean, a lot of people's attitude is, 'Look, you're successful, you have money, what do you have to be angry about?'"[60]

Lee's next film, *Girl 6* (1996), in many ways represented the low point of his film career. It is a comedy about an actress, played by Theresa Randle, who takes a job as a phone-sex operator when she cannot pay her bills. It was the first time since *She's Gotta Have It* that Lee had featured a female lead, but the film, and especially Lee's treatment of his female characters, was generally deemed shallow and sexist. It was a critical and box office failure—it made less than $5 million—with one commentator calling it Lee's worst movie. The prolific director moved on to another film.

Get on the Bus

Get on the Bus, released in 1996, represented another change in direction for the filmmaker. It was inspired by the Million Man March, which had taken place the previous year, in which hundreds of thousands of African American men had gathered in Washington, D.C., to recommit themselves to faith and family. Lee's fictional treatment follows a group of men from many different backgrounds, who board a bus in Los Angeles as strangers and arrive at the march in Washington as friends. The characters represent the wide diversity of black men in America, including a Black Muslim, a gay couple, a juvenile delinquent and his father, a cop, and a Republican. On their journey, they talk about the many issues facing African Americans, including what it means to be a father, a husband, and a man, as well as about politics, religion, and, of course, race.

Lee assembled an outstanding cast, featuring Ossie Davis, Andre Braugher, Bernie Mac, and Charles Dutton, who were widely praised for their performances. *Get on the Bus* received many positive reviews, with Todd McCarthy of *Variety* calling it "a vital regeneration of a filmmaker's talent as well as a bracing and often very funny dramatization of urgent sociopolitical themes."[61]

The film was financed by a group of successful black businessmen from several fields, including actors Wesley Snipes, Danny Glover, and Will Smith, Black Entertainment Television (BET) owner Bob Johnson, and attorney Johnnie Cochran. Lee shot the film in just eighteen days, with a budget of $2.4 million. But because it had only limited distribution and appeared in a relatively small number of theaters, the box office receipts were not substantial.

4 Little Girls

Lee's next film represented another departure for him. The movie *4 Little Girls* (1997) is a documentary recounting the harrowing story of four young girls killed in a church bombing in Birmingham, Alabama, in 1963. The bombing, by the Ku Klux Klan, was a pivotal event in the civil rights movement, one that galvanized support from blacks and whites alike for the fight for racial equality. Lee's direction was widely praised, especially his restraint in handling such a volatile and painful piece of African American history. The movie details the events leading up to and following the bombing and is interspersed with archival footage and interviews with the families of the murdered children.

Stanley Crouch, who had roundly criticized such earlier Lee films as *Do the Right Thing*, praised the documentary. In describing the effect the parents' comments had on Lee, Crouch

IN MEMORY OF

DENISE MC NAIR   CYNTHIA WESLEY ADDIE MAE COLLINS CAROL ROBERTS

THEIR LIVES WERE TAKEN BY UNKNOWN PARTIES ON SEPTEMBER 15 1963 WHEN THE SIXTEENTH STREET BAPTIST CHURCH WAS BOMBED.

"MAY MEN LEARN TO REPLACE BITTERNESS AND VIOLENCE WITH LOVE AND UNDERSTANDING"

Lee's 1997 documentary on the murder of four girls in a 1963 Birmingham, Alabama, church bombing was nominated for an Oscar.

told *New Yorker* critic John Colapinto, "There was something about the dignity of those people he encountered when he was making *4 Little Girls* that had a deep impact on him, and in some ways they seemed to help him grow up."[62]

The documentary won wide praise for Lee. Janet Maslin in the *New York Times* called it "a thoughtful, graceful, quietly devastating account,"[63] and Edward Guthmann in the *San Francisco Examiner* said it "brilliantly captures a moment in American history and tells an achingly painful story of injustice and family loss."[64] The film won Lee an Academy Award nomination for best documentary. When it did not win, Lee's reaction was typical of his previous responses when excluded from mainstream awards. The winning entry was a documentary about a group who tried to save Jewish children from the Nazi deathcamps. Lee's caustic comment was, "When I found out that one of the [nominated] films was about the Holocaust, I knew we lost."[65]

More Controversy

While Lee's tone in *4 Little Girls* indicated emotional restraint, his public pronouncements on race added to his reputation for controversy. He openly criticized acclaimed filmmaker Quentin Tarantino for his use of the word *nigger* in his films. Lee had first raised the issue in response to accusations of homophobia in his treatment of gay characters in his 1995 film *Clockers*, questioning why Tarantino was not accused of racism for his treatment of black characters. By 1997 the confrontation had become more public. Lee chastised Tarantino for his use of the

Is Spike Lee a Racist?

Lee has been accused of hating white people almost since he began making films. From *The Answer*, his earliest attempt at film in graduate school, to his most recent movies, he has been labeled a racist, with some commentators and viewers convinced that Lee's message is one of hatred of the white race.

Lee, in typical fashion, is both baffled and furious at the charge. This is what he says in his defense:

"You know what's frustrating? Ignorance. Like white people asking, why does Spike hate white people? That's ignorant to me. My films deal with the problems blacks have as well, but it always comes back to the silly notion of me hating white people, no matter what I do."

Spike Lee, interview in *Newsweek*, October 2, 2000, p. 75.

word in *Pulp Fiction* and especially in *Jackie Brown*, stating, "I have a definite problem with Quentin Tarantino's excessive use of the N-word. . . . He says he grew up on Blaxploitation films and that they were his favorite films but he has to realize that those films do not speak to the breadth of the entire African-American experience. I mean the guy's just stupid."[66]

When Tarantino was defended by Samuel L. Jackson, who had appeared in *Jackie Brown* and other Tarantino films, as well as in a number of Lee's films, Lee accused him of sounding like a "House Negro defending the master."[67] The feud between the two directors has surfaced at other times, too, and has become a source of exasperation for Lee. In his many pronouncements on the subject, he makes clear that he respects Tarantino as a talented director but also that he believes unequivocally that Tarantino's use of the "n-word" is simply not acceptable to him or to other African Americans.

A Book and a Movie About His Passion: Basketball

Amid all the controversy about his films, Lee managed to add another genre to his credits: memoirist. In 1997 he published *Best Seat in the House: A Basketball Memoir*. The book was warmly praised for its engaging look at the world of pro basketball; the players—especially Lee's beloved New York Knicks—coaches, and fans who have made the game such an important part of his life. Lee's memoir also includes many interviews with hoop stars and their devoted followers, including that other iconic Knicks fan, filmmaker Woody Allen. Lee seems especially drawn to coaches, whose work he says is similar to film directing. Although he does not court controversy in the book, Lee does discuss race, especially the predominance of African Americans in basketball, and what it means to the game and to the structure of pro sports.

In 1998 Lee explored basketball in a film, *He Got Game*, a movie that reunited him with Denzel Washington and focused on the world of big-time college sports. Washington plays a convicted felon, Jake Shuttlesworth, who is offered a week's furlough if he will convince his teenage son, Jesus, to sign with a major university to play on their basketball team. In an inspired bit of casting, Lee chose pro athlete Ray Allen, a young NBA player, for the role of Jesus.

Lee wrote the screenplay for the movie, his first original script in eight years. He focused the story on the relationship between the estranged father and son as well as on the lure of fame and fortune in sports. The movie follows one week in the life of Jesus, the number one high school basketball player in the country, as he tries to make major decisions about his future. Lee highlights the exploitation of young African Americans in athletics, at the hands of parents, schools, the media, and the professional leagues. "Everybody is trying to exploit Jesus," Lee said in an interview in *Entertainment Weekly.* "If you look at how these kids are exploited, it's cars, money, gold, and women."[68] The movie also reveals Lee's knowledge and love of the game.

He Got Game was generally well received. The response of Emmanuel Levy of *Variety* was similar to that of many commentators: "Lacking the moral indignation and militant politics of Lee's former work, this vibrantly colorful father-son melodrama is soft at the center, but it's one of the most accessible films Lee has made and Denzel Washington is terrific."[69] Yet it wasn't a great success at the box office, bringing in about $20 million, less than Lee, and his financial backers, had expected.

Summer of Sam

In 1999 Lee released his next film, *Summer of Sam*, which represented another major departure for him. Its subject was the summer of 1977, when New York City was terrorized by serial killer David Berkowitz, known as the Son of Sam. Lee directed a mostly white cast that included John Leguizamo, Mira Sorvino, Adrien Brody, and Jennifer Esposito. He based his screenplay, which he wrote with actor Michael Imperioli, on his own memories of that summer, trying to capture the temper of the times in those hot, frenzied days. Lee recalled that he had just finished his sophomore year of college and could not find a job. "I had gotten a Super 8 camera, so I spent the whole summer just going around

New York City and filming stuff." Lee also targets the media's coverage of the story, which, he claimed, "contributed to the frenzy and the mayhem that was gripping the city at the time."[70]

The movie, praised as "excellent" by Martin Scorsese, was widely panned, with critics complaining that the film was too long, bombastic, and incoherent. Andrew Sarris in the *New York*

Observer wrote, "This is trashy exploitation at its clumsiest. Once more, a Spike Lee movie has been undone by the earnestness of being important."[71] In the *Los Angeles Times*, Kenneth Turan noted, "Lee is a powerful filmmaker who certainly knows how to have an impact on an audience, but those who survive his ministrations are likely to wonder if in this case the battle was worth the bruises."[72] The movie failed at the box office, too, and was another financial disappointment for Lee. Yet his artistic energy never failed him, and he entered the new century with the release of another contentious work.

Bamboozled

Lee's 2000 film *Bamboozled*, a satire on the racist portrayal of African Americans in the media, was as controversial as any movie he had made. Written and directed by Lee, it tells the story of a Harvard-educated black television writer, Pierre Delacroix, who, when told to "dig deep into your pain" by his white boss, comes up with a new idea: an old-fashioned "Negro minstrel show," with black performers, in black face. To his horror, the show,

In Bamboozled Lee released a scathing satire on racist portrayals of African Americans in the media. It was one of his more controversial movies.

which highlights every negative black stereotype, is a huge hit, especially with white audiences.

The movie starred Damon Wayans as Delacroix, with Jada Pinkett Smith as his assistant, and dancer Savion Glover as a homeless man who becomes part of the minstrel cast. The soundtrack, produced by the musical arm of 40 Acres and a Mule, featured Stevie Wonder, Erykah Badu, and other major African American performers. Lee has said that part of the satire of the movie was aimed at gangsta rap, which he feels "has evolved to a modern day minstrel show."[73]

Most critics felt that the work was over the top and that it failed as effective satire. James Berardinelli of *Reelviews* concluded, "Lee's heavy-handed approach turns *Bamboozled* into a tedious and overlong polemic. This is sledgehammer satire."[74] Some, however, thought that the movie was vintage Spike Lee. Kenneth Turan stated in the *Los Angeles Times*, "Savage, abrasive, audacious and confrontational, *Bamboozled* is the work of a master provocateur, someone who insists audiences think about issues of race and racism we'd rather not face, especially when we go to the movies. It's the angriest film an unfailingly angry filmmaker has yet made, skewering almost everyone in it, both black and white."[75] The film was a financial disappointment, however, bringing in just over $2 million at the box office.

The Original Kings of Comedy

Within months of *Bamboozled*, Lee released *The Original Kings of Comedy*, a film version of the hugely successful comedy stage show featuring four major black comedians, Steve Harvey, D.L. Hughley, Cedric the Entertainer, and Bernie Mac. Lee noted in an interview with *Salon* that he made the film to let a wider audience know about these famed performers. "The Original Kings of Comedy were selling out arenas, not little dumpy comedy clubs; they were filling 20,000 seats. And they still weren't even being reviewed. They were totally ignored,"[76] Lee complained. The film represented a return to commercial success for Lee, bringing in more than $38 million.

Marriage and Family

During a time of ups and downs in his professional life, Lee's personal life blossomed. In 1992, he met attorney Tonya Lewis at the Black Congressional Caucus in Washington, D.C. Lee claims that he was smitten from the first moment he saw her. Finding out she was not attached, he claims he "did a little jig." They were married a year later, with Stevie Wonder singing at their wedding.

The Lee family soon grew to include two children: a daughter, Satchel (for baseball great Satchel Paige), born in 1994, and a son, Jackson, born in 1997. Their experiences as parents inspired

Spike Lee and his family arrive at a Broadway opening event. Left to right are wife Tonya, daughter Satchel, Spike Lee, and son Jackson.

Spike and Tonya Lee to write several children's books, including *Please, Baby, Please*, featuring feisty children very similar to their own.

During the first decade of the twenty-first century, Lee continued to pursue outlets for his creativity and ambition. He expanded his influence in his Brooklyn community as a philanthropist, offering academic tutoring, basketball clinics, and classes on filmmaking to residents. He continued to make successful and engaging ads, developing a partnership with an established ad agency that gave him greater creative control and more revenue. And he continued to make movies, including his greatest box office success, as well as a searing documentary about Hurricane Katrina and its aftermath. These critical and financial successes confirmed his place among the top directors of his generation.

Chapter 5

New Businesses, New Movies, and a Stunning Documentary

During the first decade of the new century, Lee continued to expand his professional life beyond movies, expanding his businesses, making music videos, working on a clothing line, creating an advertising partnership, and reaching out to members of his own Brooklyn community as an entrepreneur, philanthropist, and educator. He has also continued to direct and produce movies—including a stunning documentary—some of which are devoted to the African American experience, some featuring a different milieu.

Expanded Business Ventures

While Lee's fortunes as a filmmaker have ebbed at times, he has made several smart business decisions, forming successful partnerships and creating products with a worldwide appeal. Many of these are directly related to his skills behind the camera and to his love of music.

In the late 1980s, Lee started a musical arm of 40 Acres and a Mule: 40 Acres and a Mule Musicworks. It began with a soundtrack for *School Daze* and continued over the years, with its greatest success coming with the soundtrack to *Crooklyn*, which is "jam-packed with music from the 70s,"[77] Lee recalls. He wanted young African Americans to learn about their musical heritage, from jazz and the blues to hip-hop. He had long been a critic of the glamorized version of the black ghetto experience

Lee opened his Spike's Joint clothing boutique in Brooklyn in 1990.

in gangsta rap, and wanted to promote a more positive image for African Americans through music. He hosted a PBS show, *Spike and Company—Do It A Cappella*, directed by his longtime cinematographer Ernest Dickerson, in which he showcased the wide-ranging talents of the stars of the a cappella (without instrumental accompaniment) vocal style, including such groups as Take 6 and The Persuasions.

Lee's interest in music has expanded to music videos as well, which he has directed for a diverse group of musicians, including Michael Jackson, Branford Marsalis, Miles Davis, and Anita Baker. Two of the best-known videos he has directed are Naughty by Nature's "Hip-Hop-Hooray" and Arrested Development's "Revolution." The Musicworks portion of 40 Acres and a Mule is now a division of Columbia Records.

Lee also started a clothing and merchandising store, Spike's Joint, in 1990, and certain of its products, like the baseball cap with an embroidered "X," to promote the movie *Malcolm X*, became tremendously popular. After several years, however, the retail shops became too time-consuming and distracting, and he closed them. "It was just a full-time thing, retail, and I wanted to concentrate on filmmaking,"[78] he said.

Lee continues to be involved in the clothing business through an agreement with New Era Cap Company, the official on-field cap for Major League Baseball. A longtime New York Yankees fan, Lee has collaborated with New Era on a number of baseball caps, most recently in 2009, when the company announced a new Yankee-inspired hat, called "Spike Lee Joint 2.0." Lee says the hat was inspired by the team's long dominance of major league ball: "It seemed fitting that it represent the most decorated franchise in professional sports,"[79] he claims.

An Entrepreneur Who Gives Back to the Community

Lee also expanded the scope of 40 Acres and a Mule into his Brooklyn neighborhood, with an outreach program offering young people school tutoring, SAT and college prep courses, basketball camps, and the chance to learn about filmmaking. The 40 Acres and a Mule Institute offered classes in Fort Greene run by Long Island University. Lee used his contacts within the film industry to bring in some of the biggest names in moviemaking for the students. "We gave a class every Saturday morning, and each class would have a different guest. I remember Robert De Niro came, Martin Scorsese, the Hughes brothers."[80] In addition to the classes, Lee published books on each of his films, as an aid to understanding the practical, hands-on aspects of the profession. In particular, he wanted to demystify the world of filmmaking and to encourage young people to think of it as a career.

"You don't need to go to film school to be a director. It's enough to get a camera, or work on a set, and learn the craft."[81]

Spike Lee lectures on film to students at Brown University. He has also lectured at Harvard and New York University.

Lee also began lecturing on filmmaking at Harvard and New York University. At NYU, his alma mater, he teaches a course on the director's role as a leader and artist. The dean of the film school, Mary Schmidt Campbell, said this about his contribution: "He feels that part of what he is giving [his students] is access. He is a very impressive teacher. . . . I think it has to do with his sense that, in addition to the opportunity to do his work, he has a responsibility to the larger world toward the next generation and teaching is one of the tools he can use to fulfill that responsibility."[82]

Advertising

From his early ads for Nike, Lee has created highly effective—and popular—ad campaigns for a variety of products, including Levi's, the Gap, Snapple, Ben & Jerry's Ice Cream, and Diet Coke. Lee even created a character, Mars Blackmon, as something of an alter ego who for years appeared in his Nike ads with Michael Jordan.

In the late 1990s Lee announced that he was creating an advertising agency, called Spike/DDB, that he formed with the ad firm DDB Needham. They wanted him to help them reach an important emerging market: urban young adults, with an interest in fashion and music. Lee was happy with the new direction, which has allowed him greater control over the advertising he creates, and, because he now owns 51 percent of the company, greater revenue, too.

His shrewd insights into the business show the keen mind of an experienced businessman. "When I do commercials, I know that it is the client's word that counts at the end: they present you with the idea, the storyboards are there, and you just execute it. I really wanted to have more of a hold on the creative thing."

Spike Lee: That's My Story and I'm Sticking To It, as told to Kaleem Aftab. New York: Norton, 2006, p.288.

Lee jokes with Miami Heat player Dwayne Wade during a commercial shoot for Converse shoes. Lee has shown a shrewd acumen for business.

Major Movies of the Decade

Lee also continued to add memorable movies to his ever-expanding opus of films. Some returned to familiar topics, while others represented new directions for him. And he added another documentary to his list of credits, a work that became one of his most critically successful films.

His first successful movie of the twenty-first century was 25th Hour, released in 2002. It was a major departure for him, in topic and tone. Set in New York City, it tells the story of Monty Brogan (played by Ed Norton), who is spending his last night of freedom before reporting to prison to serve a seven-year sentence for selling drugs. The film follows him as he says goodbye to his father, his girlfriend, and his best friends, while confronting his own demons and trying to make peace with his past. The movie is based on a novel by David Benioff, who also wrote the screenplay. Lee made the film after the terrorist attacks of September 11, 2001, and the spirit of that tragedy informs the entire movie. The tone is somber, almost elegiac. The film begins with a panoramic shot of the New York skyline, and a plane passing through the light mural of the Twin Towers, a vision of remembrance and loss. Lee emphasizes the dislocated, despairing emotional states of his characters through use of his signature dolly shot, in scenes that depict characters drifting above the ground, wounded and grieving, like specters.

Unlike most of Lee's films, the cast is predominantly white. It features outstanding performances by Philip Seymour Hoffman, Rosario Dawson, and Anna Paquin. Commentators especially praised Norton's performance. CNN film critic Paul Clinton noted that "Norton and Lee make a great team. Both men are excellent storytellers and both share an emotional honesty that shines through on screen."[83]

The movie was a financial success for Lee. It brought in about $24 million in worldwide revenue, doing well in the United States and overseas. It was a critical success, too, with critics and audiences alike praising the movie for its insightful portrait of a man, and a city, dealing with fear and with fate. In the Washington Post, Ann Hornaday noted, "With supreme control and restraint—two qualities the director hasn't always exhibited even in his finest work up to now—Lee delves deeply into Monty's shame and self-loathing. . . . In the startling, unforgettable masterstroke that concludes the movie, Lee starts out by paying homage to one man's home town, but he slowly turns that gesture into a hymn to America, in all its restless energy and outlaw spirit, its love of reinvention and its seductive, elusive dreams. With the small story of a relatively seedy character, Lee has created that rarity in filmmaking: a movie we need, right now."[84]

Inside Man

Lee's next major film, *Inside Man*, was released in 2006. A thriller about a bank heist, it features three famous actors, Denzel Washington as an New York City Police Department hostage negotiator, Clive Owen as a bank robber, and Jodie Foster as a high-powered businesswoman.

The film came out of the Imagine Entertainment studios, which is run by two of Hollywood's most important and influential media figures, Ron Howard and Brian Grazer. Despite the ups and downs of Lee's career, they were sure of his talent: "What mattered to me was that in every movie, whether it was *Bamboozled* or *Malcolm X* or *Do the Right Thing*, he always shot good scenes," recalled Grazer. There remained the issue of Lee's notoriously prickly nature. "There are executives within the establishment that felt, 'Hey, we're not sure we wanna hire Spike Lee,'"[85] said Grazer. But he and Howard were sure, and Lee went on to make them a great, and financially successful, film.

Inside Man was much more than a typical cops-and-robbers movie. Lee added material to the original screenplay, by Russell Gerwitz, details about race, class, New York politics, and finance, that were, in the opinion of critics, seamlessly woven into the story, enlarging and enriching the film.

The movie was a great success for Lee, winning wide praise from commentators and taking in more than $176 million at the box office, making it the biggest financial success of his career. Critics were especially impressed by the way that Lee brought wit and depth to an old Hollywood genre, the bank

Lee discusses an upcoming scene with Denzel Washington on the Inside Man *set. Lee received high praise from critics, and the film made $176 million at the box office.*

heist movie. Lou Lumenick of the *New York Post* called it "a crackling, twisty thriller about a bank heist that shows [Lee] can make an expensive, mainstream movie that's every bit as well-crafted as the personal, arty films to which he has devoted most of his career."[86] David Ansen of *Newsweek* agreed, noting, "As unexpected as some of its plot twists is the fact that this unapologetic genre movie was directed by Spike Lee, who has never sold himself as Mr. Entertainment. But here it is, a Spike Lee joint that's downright fun."[87]

When the Levees Broke

The same year that *Inside Man* became a box office hit, Lee released a four-hour documentary for HBO that chronicled the disaster of Hurricane Katrina and the inept government response to it. *When the Levees Broke: A Requiem in Four Acts*, is a devastating look at what happened after Katrina destroyed most of New Orleans in

2005. Lee filmed the series over six months, visiting the city nine times and interviewing more than one hundred residents, many of them from the mostly African American lower Ninth Ward, where the hurricane did most of its damage.

Lee tells his story through those interviews, as well as with archival and amateur footage and stills. The heartfelt music of Terence Blanchard is woven throughout the film. Blanchard, a New Orleans native, offers a personal perspective on the disaster, too. Lee films him taking his mother back to her neighborhood after the water had receded and documents her horror and grief as she sees the ruins of her home.

Several scenes stand out because of their power and eloquence. One of the subjects, an African American woman named Phyllis Montana LeBlanc, turns the full force of her fury at the government while Lee's camera is rolling, at once eloquent

Lee attends a press conference about his film When the Levees Broke. *Despite controversy the film garnered three Emmys, a Peabody, and two Venice Film Festival awards.*

in her anger and searingly funny in her depiction of government inaction. Another scene of horror and grief plays out at the Superdome sports arena, where an elderly woman died in her wheelchair after waiting for hours for the buses that were to evacuate the citizens of the city.

"No one who sees the film will come away unaffected," predicted *Houston Chronicle* film critic Eric Harrison, and that prediction proved prophetic. The work won nearly universal praise from critics, with Harrison concluding that "even more than *Do the Right Thing*, until now Lee's major achievement, *When the Levees Broke* is simultaneously his most searing and topical movie and the one most assured of enduring."[88] David Denby of the *New Yorker* concurred, claiming that "anyone hoping to reclaim Katrina emotionally—to experience what the city went through in all its phases of loss, anger, and contempt—needs to see Lee's movie, which is surely the most magnificent and large-souled record of a great American tragedy ever put on film."[89]

The film was not without its controversies, however. Lee included the comments of some New Orleans residents who claimed that they had heard explosions near the Ninth Ward, suggesting that the levees had been purposely dynamited by the government. While Lee says he presented these views, as well as contrary opinions, for balance, he did come under fire for including them. Fueling the fire, Lee had this to say in the commentary section of the DVD: "Many African-Americans—and I include myself in this group—don't put anything past the United States government when it comes to black people."[90] Still, the movie stands as one of his most important achievements in cinema. It won three Emmys, a Peabody, and two awards at the Venice Film Festival. In 2010 HBO announced that Lee would be producing a follow-up documentary on the tragedy.

Miracle at St. Anna

Lee's next major movie was *Miracle at St. Anna* (2008), a historical film based on a novel by James McBride that tells the story of the all-black Ninety-second Infantry Division of the U.S.

Army, which fought in Italy in World War II. The film focuses on these "Buffalo Soldiers" (as all-black army units were called in nineteenth-century America), centering in particular on four men who become separated from their unit near a small village in Tuscany. One of the soldiers, Sam Train (played by Omar Benson Miller) becomes close to a little boy from the village, a relationship meant to show the human bond that can transcend race and war.

Even before the movie was released, Lee became embroiled in controversy on the topic of blacks in films about World War II. He engaged in an open battle of words with director Clint Eastwood, whom he criticized for not including black soldiers in either of his recent war epics, *Letters from Iwo Jima* and *Flags of Our Fathers*. When Eastwood angrily suggested that "a guy like that should shut his face," Lee replied that "the man is not my father, and we're not on a plantation either." He made it clear that part of his motivation in making the movie was to make audiences

On the Power of Film

Spike Lee has always been a "teacher" of film. In the classroom—but mostly outside of it—in his books, and in the "language" of the film medium, he tries to help people recognize the power of the image, from a social, political, and personal point of view.

"I want people to think about the power of images, not just in terms of race, but how imagery is used and what sort of social impact it has—how it influences how we talk, how we think, how we view one another. In particular, I want them to see how film and television have historically, from the birth of both mediums, produced and perpetuated and distorted images. Film and television started out that way, and here we are, at the dawn of a new century, and a lot of that madness is still with us today."

Spike Lee, interview in *Cineaste*, January 2001, p.9.

aware of the contributions of African Americans in the Second World War. "If you look at the history of World War II in films, we're invisible," he claimed in an interview with John Colapinto of the *New Yorker*. "We're omitted."[91]

Despite the war of words and ensuing controversy, the movie failed to gain an audience and was a critical and box office disappointment for Lee. Many commentators dismissed it as a failure, citing its length, convoluted plot, and plodding pace. Some wondered how Lee could have made such a misstep, especially after the brilliance of *When the Levees Broke*. Ann Hornaday of the *Washington Post* wrote, "Overwrought, overproduced, overbusy and overlong, *Miracle at St. Anna* finally suffers from the worst filmmaking sin of all: the failure of trust, in the story and the audience."[92]

The Presidential Campaign of Barack Obama

The year 2008 was not without its bright spots, however, as Lee turned his energies to the presidential campaign of Barack Obama, whose election he saw as a chance for America to truly take a step forward in race relations. "If we have a black President, maybe it will change people's psyches," he said in the *New Yorker* interview with John Colapinto. "This thing is not by accident," he said of Obama's candidacy. "I think this thing is ordained—it's providence. This is a sweeping movement. It's bigger than him, it's bigger than all of us."[93]

Lee was exasperated by the way Obama's race was handled by the mainstream media. In response to a *Time* magazine story titled "Is Obama Black Enough?" Lee spoke for the candidate and himself, defying anyone to define either of them by their race. "It's ignorance. Here's the thing. I'm not one of those people who're going to be defined by the ghetto mentality, that you have to have been shot, have numerous babies from many women, be ignorant, getting high all the time, walking around with pants hanging from your ass—and that's a black man? I'm not buying that. That's not my definition."[94]

Lee films history as he watches president-elect Barack Obama give a speech at Grant Park in Chicago on the night of his election to the presidency.

After Obama won, Lee had this to say about the future for African Americans: "Some people want to act like we've been delivered, like there is no more racism, no more prejudice. That's not the case at all. So we have to stay vigilant. We live in a time where some young black men say they're okay with the fact that they might not live past 18 years old. Any time young black men think like that, you know, something is wrong. We're killing each other. It's genocide and a lot of it is fueled by many factors. But we have to stop it if we are going to survive as a people."[95]

Lee has used the term "genocide" to describe the fate of far too many African American young people. Speaking at the University of Memphis in 2010, he talked about "young ignorant black kids failing class on purpose because if you speak correct English, (if) you get A's, then somehow that means you're a sellout. This is something we have to stop because it's genocide."[96] He's used the term to describe the corrosive effect of gangsta rap on young people as well. "I don't know why we were glorifying drug dealers. It's the same thing with this gangsta rap—you know, the glorification of "thuggery" and gangsters. These hip-hop guys boast how many times they have seen *Scarface*. It's crazy. It is really leading to our demise."[97]

Passing Strange

Lee's next film, 2009's *Passing Strange*, represented another departure for the director. It was based on the Broadway hit of the same name, by the musician and actor Stew. It chronicles the life of a young African American called Youth from adolescence to adulthood as he pursues the "real life." "Adulthood is the consequence of decisions made by a teenager," states Stew, playing the role of the Narrator. He leads the audience from his middle-class upbringing in Los Angeles, which he finds sterile and fake, to a world of drugs and punk rock, on to Europe and further exploration, always in search of a truer existence, in life and in music.

Lee had attended the opening night of the stage version of *Passing Strange* in New York City, and he was determined to film it. He and cinematographer Matty Libatique studied the show carefully, and Lee saw it about sixteen times: "Twice for the public, four times on Broadway, and after I knew I was going to do it, probably another ten times." The scenes were shot at three different performances at the Belasco Theater on Broadway, including closing night. Lee recalled that the crew used fourteen cameras to film the play, in their effort to "tell the story. What angles best conveyed what we needed in that moment."[98]

The result was a film that won Lee nearly universal praise. A.O. Scott in the *New York Times* thought the film version was even better than the Broadway show, because, through a combination of shots, angles, and editing, Lee provided a focus for the viewer that the theatrical version lacked. "Loose ends ceased to dangle; soft spots were smoothed away and slow passages tightened up," Scott claimed. "The camera movements and compositions immerse the viewer at once in the story and the process of the performance." The result is a show "not simply preserved by Mr. Lee's camera, but brought, somehow, to its fullest, strangest, most electrifying realization."[99]

In late 2009 Lee was once again embroiled in a controversy with another film director, but this time, the other director was also black. Lee openly criticized the successful films and television shows of director Tyler Perry, saying, "There's a lot of stuff out today that is coonery and buffoonery. I see ads for [Perry's television shows] 'Meet the Browns' and 'House of Payne' and I'm scratching my head. We've got a black president and we're going back[ward]. The image is troubling and it harkens back to 'Amos 'n' Andy.'"[100] Perry was quick to respond, calling Lee's comments "insulting" during an interview on *60 Minutes*. Perry continued, "It's attitudes like that that make Hollywood think that these people [his characters] do not exist and that's why there's no material speaking to them, speaking to us. I would love to read that to my fan base."[101] The feud is still unresolved, and is only the most recent example of Lee's unreserved frankness and willingness to court controversy, unchanged from his earliest work.

Today, Spike Lee is widely acknowledged to be the most important African American filmmaker in the nation, still able to capture audiences, to ignite controversy, and to inspire admiration for his films. Currently, Lee is working on several film projects that he has been hoping to do for years now, including biographical profiles of three great African American legends: baseball great Jackie Robinson, boxing great Joe Louis, and singing sensation James Brown. Lee's muse as well as his ambition indicate that he will continue to be a force in the movie world for decades to come, seeking to define the African American experience, but never to be defined by anything other than his own vision.

Chapter 1: Becoming Spike

1. Quoted in John Colapinto, "Outside Man," *New Yorker*, September 22, 2008. www.newyorker.com/reporting/2008/09/22/080922fa_fact_colapinto.
2. Quoted in Kaleem Aftab, *Spike Lee: That's My Story and I'm Sticking To It*. New York: Norton, 2006, p. 9.
3. Quoted in Colapinto, "Outside Man."
4. Quoted in Gerri Hirshey, "Spike's Peak," *Vanity Fair*, June 1991, pp. 90–92.
5. Quoted in Aftab, *Spike Lee*, p. 14.
6. Quoted in Aftab, *Spike Lee*, p. 15.
7. Quoted in Aftab, *Spike Lee*, p. 20.
8. Quoted in Aftab, *Spike Lee*, p. 22.
9. Quoted in Colapinto, "Outside Man."
10. Quoted in Colapinto, "Outside Man."
11. Quoted in Colapinto, "Outside Man."
12. Quoted in Colapinto, "Outside Man."
13. Quoted in Hirshey, "Spike's Peak," pp. 70, 80-92.
14. Quoted in Colapinto, "Outside Man."
15. Quoted in Colapinto, "Outside Man."
16. Quoted in Colapinto, "Outside Man."

Chapter 2: *Do the Right Thing*

17 Quoted in Marlaine Glicksman,"Spike Lee's Bed-Stuy BBQ," *Film Comment*, July/August 1989, p. 12.
18. Quoted in George Khoury, "Big Words: An Interview with Spike Lee," *Creative Screenwriting,* May/June 1999, p. 41.
19. From *Do the Right Thing*, by Spike Lee, 1989.
20. Quoted in Arts and Leisure, *New York Times*, June 25, 1989, p. 21.
21. Quoted in James S. Kunen, "Spike Lee Inflames the Critics with a Film He Swears Is the Right Thing," *People*, July 10, 1989. www.people.com/people/archive/article/0,201207 18,00.

22. Quoted in Colapinto, "Outside Man."
23. Stanley Crouch, "Do the Race Thing," *Village Voice,* June 20, 1989, p. 73.
24. Vincent Canby, "Spike Lee Tackles Racism in *Do the Right Thing,* June 30, 1989. www.nytimes.com/1989/06/30/movies/review.
25. Roger Ebert, *"Do the Right Thing,"* *Chicago Sun-Times,* June 30, 1989. http://rogerebert.suntimes.com/apps/pbcs.dll/article?AID=/19890630/REVIEWS/906300301/1023.
26. Quoted in Aftab, *Spike Lee,* p. 103.
27. Quoted in Glicksman, "Spike Lee's Bed-Stuy BBQ," p. 16.
28. Quoted in Glicksman, "Spike Lee's Bed-Stuy BBQ," p. 14.
29. Richard Brody, "New York, New York," *New Yorker,* April 17, 2006. www.newyorker.com/archive/2006/04/17/060 417gomo_GOAT_movies1.

Chapter 3: Race, Politics, and Personal Relationships

30. Quoted in Aftab, *Spike Lee,* p. 129.
31. Quoted in Lynn Norment, "'Mo' Better Blues': Backstage with Spike Lee and the Cast," *Ebony,* September 1990, p. 30.
32. Caryn James, "Spike Lee's Middle-Class Jazz Musician," Arts and Leisure, *New York Times,* August 3, 1990, p. 1.
33. Roger Ebert, *"Mo' Better Blues,"* *Chicago Sun Times,* August 3, 1990, p. 29.
34. Spike Lee, "I Am Not an Anti-Semite," Arts and Leisure, *New York Times,* August 22, 1990, p. 3.
35. Spike Lee, "I Am Not an Anti-Semite," Arts and Leisure, *New York Times,* August 22, 1990, p. 3.
36. Quoted in Janice Mosier Richolson, "He's Gotta Have It: An Interview with Spike Lee," *Cineaste,* vol. 18, no. 4, 1991, p. 12.
37. Quoted in Richolson, "He's Gotta Have It," p.14.
38. Desson Howe, *"Jungle Fever,"* Arts, *Washington Post,* June 7, 1991, p. 1.
39. Roger Ebert, *"Jungle Fever,"* *Chicago Sun-Times,* June 7, 1991. http://rogerebert.suntimes.com/apps/pbcs.dll/article?AID=/ 19910607/REVIEWS/106070305/1023.
40. Howe, *"Jungle Fever,"* p. 1.

41. Quoted in Richolson, "He's Gotta Have It," p. 12.
42. Quoted in Richolson, "He's Gotta Have It," p. 12.
43. *Jet*, "Spike Lee Falls Out with Jazzman Dad Bill Lee over Mixed Marriage," May 16, 1994, p. 56.
44. Quoted in Colapinto, "Outside Man."
45. Quoted in Gary Crowdus and Dan Georgakas, "Our Film Is Only a Starting Point: An Interview with Spike Lee," *Cineaste*, vol. 19, no. 4, 1993, p. 22.
46. Quoted in Aftab, *Spike Lee*, p. 180.
47. Quoted in Aftab, *Spike Lee*, p. 181.
48. Quoted in Crowdus and Georgakas, "Our Film Is Only a Starting Point," p. 21.
49. Quoted in Crowdus and Georgakas, "Our Film Is Only a Starting Point," p. 21.
50. Quoted in Crowdus and Georgakas, "Our Film Is Only a Starting Point," p. 22.
51. Quoted in Aftab, *Spike Lee*, p. 181.
52. Quoted in Aftab, *Spike Lee*, p. 182.
53. Peter Travers, "*Malcolm X*," *Rolling Stone*, November 20, 1992, p. 75.
54. Terrence Rafferty, "*Malcolm X*," *New Yorker*, 1992. www.newyorker.com/arts/reviews/film/malcolm_x_lee?.
55. Vincent Canby, "*Malcolm X*, as Complex as Its Subject," Arts and Leisure, *New York Times*, November 18, 1992, p. 1.

Chapter 4: A Change in Direction

56. Spike Lee, interviewed by Charlie Rose, *The Charlie Rose Show*, June 17, 1994, www.charlierose.com/guest/view/322.
57. Quoted in Aftab, *Spike Lee*, p. 228.
58. Janet Maslin, "A Tender Domestic Drama from, No Joke, Spike Lee," Arts and Leisure, *New York Times*, May 13, 1994, p. 1.
59. Spike Lee, interviewed by Charlie Rose.
60. Spike Lee, interviewed by Anna Deveare Smith, *Premiere*, October 1995. www.tcm.com/tcmdb/participant.jsp?spid=111142&apid=0.
61. Todd McCarthy, "*Get On the Bus*," *Variety*, October 7, 1996. www.variety.com/review/VE1117905658.html?categoryid=31&cs=1.

62. Quoted in Colapinto, "Outside Man."

63. Janet Maslin, "Still Reeling from the Day Death Came to Birmingham," Arts and Leisure, *New York Times,* July 9, 1997, p. 1.

64. Edward Guthmann, "Lee Shows the Tragedy of *4 Little Girls, San Francisco Chronicle,* October 10, 1997, p. C3.

65. Quoted in Colapinto, "Outside Man."

66. Quoted in George Khoury, "Big Words: An Interview with Spike Lee," *Creative Screenwriting,* May/June 1999, p. 39.

67. Quoted in Colapinto, "Outside Man."

68. Quoted in Chris Nasawaty, "Hoops to Conquer," *Entertainment Weekly,* May 22, 1998, p. 46.

69. Emmanuel Levy, *"He Got Game,"* *Variety,* April 27, 1998. www.variety.com/review/VE1117477426.html?categoryid= 31&cs=1&query=he+got+game.

70. Quoted in Stephen Pizzello, "Spike Lee's Seventies Flashback," *American Cinematographer,* June 1999, p. 51.

71. Andrew Sarris, *"Summer of Sam,"* *New York Observer,* July 11, 1999. www.observer.com/node/41715.

72. Kenneth Turan, *"Summer of Sam,"* *Los Angeles Times,* July 2, 1999. www.calendarlive.com/movies/reviews/cl-movie9907 01-3,0,6006141.story.

73. Quoted in Michael Sragow, "Black like Spike," *Salon,* October 26, 2000. http://dir.salon.com/ent/col/srag/2000/10/ 26/spike_lee/index.html?sid=990028.

74. James Berardinelli, *"Bamboozled,"* in *Reelviews,* October 2000. www.reelviews.net/movies/b/bamboozled.html.

75. Kenneth Turan, "Satire, Rage Add Up to Audacious *Bamboozled,"* *Los Angeles Times,* October 6, 2000. www.calendarlive .com/movies/reviews/cl-movie001005-8,0,4372327.story.

76. Quoted in Sragow, "Black like Spike."

Chapter 5: New Businesses, New Movies, and a Stunning Documentary

77. Quoted in Aftab, *Spike Lee,* p. 233.

78. Quoted in Aftab, *Spike Lee,* p. 269.

79. PR Newswire, "New Era Cap and Spike Lee to Unveil Newest Addition to the 'Spike Lee Joint' Cap Collection," September 24, 2009. www.neweracap.com/.

80. Quoted in Aftab, *Spike Lee*, p. 130.
81. Quoted in Aftab, *Spike Lee*, p. 238.
82. Quoted in Aftab, *Spike Lee*, p. 271.
83. Paul Clinton, "A Thoughtful, Timely *25th Hour,*" CNN.com, January 11, 2003. www.cnn.com/2003/SHOWBIZ/Movies/01/09/review.25th.hour/index.html.
84. Ann Hornaday, "*25th Hour*: Stunningly True to Its Time," *Washington Post*, January 10, 2003. www.washingtonpost.com/wp-dyn/content/article/2003/01/10/AR2005033116234 .html.
85. Quoted in Colapinto, "Outside Man."
86. Lou Lumenick, *"Inside Man," New York Post*, April 24, 2006. www.nypost.com/movies/65906.htm.
87. David Ansen, "All the Way to the Bank," in *Newsweek*, April 3, 2006. www.newsweek.com/id/45911.
88. Eric Harrison, "Devastation, Hope Remain," *Houston Chronicle*, August 21, 2006. www.chron.com/disp/story.mpl/ent/4129538.html.
89. David Denby, "Disasters," *New Yorker*, September 4, 2006. www.newyorker.com/archive/2006/09/04/060904crci_cinema.
90. Quoted in Colapinto, "Outside Man."
91. Quoted in Colapinto, "Outside Man."
92. Ann Hornaday, "*Miracle at St. Anna,*" *Washington Post*, September 26, 2008. www.washingtonpost.com/gog/movies/miracle-at-st.-anna,1146328.
93. Quoted in Colapinto, "Outside Man."
94. Quoted in Colapinto, "Outside Man."
95. Spike Lee, interviewed by Ed Gordon, *Business Wire*, May 28, 2009. http://newsblaze.com/story/2009052812370600001.bw/topstory.html.
96. Quoted in John Beifuss, "Spike Lee Bemoans 'Misguided Minds' of Black Youth," *Memphis Commercial Appeal*, March 18, 2010. www.commercialappeal.com/news/2010/mar/18/lee-bemoans-misguided-minds-of-black-youths/.
97. Lee, interviewed by Ed Gordon.
98. Spike Lee, interviewed by Laremy Legel, Film.com. www.film.com/celebrities/spike-lee/story/spike-lee-interview-passing-strange/25505582.

99. A.O. Scott, "A Young Artist's Journey, This Time on Film," *New York Times*, August 21, 2009. www.movies.nytimes .com/2009/08/21/movies/21passing.html.

100. Lee, interviewed by Ed Gordon.

101. Tyler Perry, quoted in an interview on *60 Minutes*, October 23, 2009. www.cbsnews.com/stories/2009/10/22/60minutes/ main5410095.

Important Dates

1957
Shelton Jackson Lee, nicknamed Spike, is born in Atlanta, Georgia, on March 20.

1959
The Lee family moves to New York; they eventually buy a house in Fort Greene, Brooklyn.

1975
Spike Lee graduates from John Dewey High School and attends Morehouse College in Atlanta, Georgia.

1977
Jacqueline Lee, Spike's mother, dies of cancer.

1979
Lee graduates from Morehouse College with a major in mass communications.

He spends the summer of 1979 working for Columbia Pictures in Los Angeles.

He begins a master of arts program in film at New York University.

1980
As his first-year film project, Lee makes *The Answer*, an attack on D.W. Griffith's *Birth of a Nation*.

1982
Lee graduates from NYU with a master's degree in film production. His senior thesis, *Joe's Bed-Stuy Barbershop: We Cut Heads*, wins the Motion Picture Arts and Sciences Student Academy Award and is screened at Lincoln Center.

1983
Lee works for a small film distribution company; begins work on first commercial movie.

1984

Lee abandons his first film project, *The Messenger*, over funding and labor issues.

1985

Lee releases his first commercial movie, *She's Gotta Have It*, which costs $175,000, and eventually makes $8 million. The film wins the Prix de la Jeunesse at the Cannes film festival.

1988

Lee releases his second movie, *School Daze*.

Lee publishes *Spike Lee's Gotta Have It: Inside Guerilla Film-making*.

He produces his first Nike ad for Air Jordan campaign, featuring Michael Jordan and Lee as Mars Blackmon.

1989

Lee releases *Do the Right Thing*; it is immediately controversial, with critics and politicians fearing it will cause rioting.

The film is nominated for Academy Awards in two categories: Best Original Screenplay (for Lee) and Best Supporting Actor (for Danny Aiello).

He starts a retail merchandising business, Spike's Joint, in New York and Los Angeles.

1990

Lee releases *Mo' Better Blues*.

1991

Lee releases *Jungle Fever*.

1992

Lee releases *Malcolm X*.

1993

Lee marries Tonya Linnette Lewis.

1994

Lee's daughter, Satchel Paige Lee, is born.

Lee releases *Crooklyn*.

1995

Lee releases *Clockers*.

1996

Lee releases *Girl 6* and *Get on the Bus*.

Lee creates new advertising firm in partnership with DDB Needham, Spike/DDB.

1997

Lee's son, Jackson, is born.

He releases *4 Little Girls*; it is nominated for an Academy Award for Best Documentary.

He publishes a memoir about his love of basketball, *Best Seat in the House*.

1998

Lee releases *He Got Game*.

1999

Lee releases *Summer of Sam*.

2000

Lee releases *The Original Kings of Comedy* and *Bamboozled*.

2002

Lee releases *25th Hour*.

With his wife, Tonya, publishes a children's book, *Please, Baby, Please*.

2006

Lee releases *Inside Man*.

Lee's HBO documentary *When the Levees Broke* airs on television; wins Lee three Emmys.

2008
Lee releases *Miracle at St. Anna.*

2009
Lee releases *Passing Strange.*

2010
Lee releases sports documentary *Kobe Doin' Work.*

For More Information

Books

Dennis Abrams, *Spike Lee: Director.* New York: Chelsea House, 2008. A young adult biography of Lee, tracing his career from its beginnings to 2008.

Kaleem Aftab, *Spike Lee: That's My Story and I'm Sticking to It.* New York: Norton, 2006. A comprehensive overview of Lee's life and career. Although it is an authorized biography, it is considered an objective and thorough analysis of Lee's life in film.

Cynthia Fuchs, ed., *Spike Lee Interviews.* Jackson: University Press of Mississippi, 2002. A wide-ranging collection of twenty-two interviews, dating from 1986 to 2002 and covering Lee's career from *She's Gotta Have It* to *Bamboozled.*

James Earl Hardy, *Spike Lee.* New York: Chelsea House, 1996. A biographical and critical introduction to Lee's life and work, written for students from middle to high school, and covering Lee's output through 1996.

John Howard, *Faces in the Mirror: Oscar Micheaux & Spike Lee.* Forest City, NC: Fireside Books, 2010. Compares and contrasts the careers of African American directors Lee and Micheaux, who was one of the first black directors in the country.

K. Maurice Jones, *Spike Lee and the African American Filmmakers: A Choice of Colors.* Brookfield, CT: Millbrook Press, 1996. Written for students grade five and above, the volume covers Lee and several other contemporary black filmmakers, noting how racial issues inform their work.

Spike Lee, *Spike Lee's Gotta Have It: Inside Guerilla Filmmaking.* New York: Fireside, 1988. The first of Lee's books based on his movies, including the script and commentary by Lee on the making of the movie. He has published similar books on many of his later films, including *Do the Right Thing* and *Malcolm X.*

Periodicals

John Colapinto, "Outside Man," *New Yorker*, September 22, 2008.

Gary Crowdus and Dan Georgakas, "Thinking About the Power of Images: An Interview with Spike Lee," *Cineaste*, January 2001.

Logan Hill, "How I Made It: Spike Lee on *Do the Right Thing*," April 7, 2008.

Internet Sources

Lee Siegel, "Spike Lee Talks about Movies, Race, and Will Smith," *Slate*, December 1, 2005. www.slate.com.

Scott Simon, "A Conversation with Spike Lee," transcript of a radio interview from *Weekend Edition*, April 1, 2006. www.npr .org/templates/story/story.php?storyId=5317036.

Michael Sragow, "Black like Spike," *Salon*, October 6, 2000. www.salon.com/entertainment/col/srag/2000/10/26/spike_le e/index.html.

Web Sites

Biography Resource Center Online, 2010 (http://galenet.gale group.com/servelt/BioRC) This online resource contains many important reference sources relating to Lee's life and work, including entries from *Authors and Artists for Young Adults, American Decades, St. James Encyclopedia of Popular Culture,* and *Notable Black American Men.*

40 Acres and a Mule (www.40acres.com) This is the official Web site of 40 Acres and a Mule Filmworks, which offers information on Lee's films of the past, present, and in production, as well as information on local and national events in film.

Gale Cengage (http://www.gale.cengage.com/free_resources/ bhm/bio/lee_s.htm) The Lee biography on this site is part of a group of free resources available to students of African American history.

Laurie Lanzen Harris has worked in publishing for thirty-three years, at Gale Research (now Gale Cengage), where she was director of the Literary Criticism Series; at Omnigraphics, where she was editorial director; and for the past ten years at Favorable Impressions, where she is president, publisher, and editor of the Biography for Beginners series of publications. She has written or edited more than one hundred books for readers from elementary school through college.